"Meg, I don't want to leave you and Travis here alone tonight."

She'd been longing to hear those words all night, but not under the present circumstances. Not under any circumstances where Ian would feel obligated to stay.

"I think we're good, Ian. We're not even sure there was ever anyone lurking around outside."

Ian's eyes narrowed to cold slits. "Why are you pushing me away, Meg? I'm not interested in sharing your bed. It's not just about you anymore. I have a son in there, and I'm here to protect him."

His words lashed her face and she dropped her head, allowing her hair to create a veil around her hot cheeks. He wanted his son but not her. "Okay, you can stay."

She jerked away from his gentle touch and pushed up from the couch. "I'll get you a blanket and pillow."

When she returned, Ian stepped over the coffee table with one long stride and enveloped her in a warm embrace. When he stroked the back of her hair, she melted against him…just a little.

"I should never have used your tour group. I never meant to drag you into my operation."

"Maybe it was fate. You discovered your son." And rediscovered he had a wife who could never admit how much she had missed him.

CAROL ERICSON

MOUNTAIN RANGER RECON

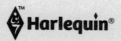

Harlequin®

TORONTO NEW YORK LONDON
AMSTERDAM PARIS SYDNEY HAMBURG
STOCKHOLM ATHENS TOKYO MILAN MADRID
PRAGUE WARSAW BUDAPEST AUCKLAND

To Angi, my sprinting partner in crime

Recycling programs
for this product may
not exist in your area.

ISBN-13: 978-0-373-69540-9

MOUNTAIN RANGER RECON

Copyright © 2011 by Carol Ericson

www.eHarlequin.com

Printed in U.S.A.

ABOUT THE AUTHOR

Carol Ericson lives with her husband and two sons in Southern California, home of state-of-the-art cosmetic surgery, wild freeway chases, palm trees bending in the Santa Ana winds and a million amazing stories. These stories, along with hordes of virile men and feisty women, clamor for release from Carol's head. It makes for some interesting headaches until she sets them free to fulfill their destinies and her readers' fantasies. To find out more about Carol, her books and her strange headaches, please visit her website at www.carolericson.com, "where romance flirts with danger."

Books by Carol Ericson

HARLEQUIN INTRIGUE
1034—THE STRANGER AND I
1079—A DOCTOR-NURSE ENCOUNTER
1117—CIRCUMSTANTIAL MEMORIES
1184—THE SHERIFF OF SILVERHILL
1231—THE MCCLINTOCK PROPOSAL
1250—A SILVERHILL CHRISTMAS
1267—NAVY SEAL SECURITY#
1273—MOUNTAIN RANGER RECON#

#Brothers in Arms

CAST OF CHARACTERS

Meg O'Reilly Dempsey—Meg enjoys her job leading mountain hikes for tourists, but when her estranged husband shows up on one of her tours bringing espionage and secrets, she realizes it's time to tell him the biggest secret of all.

Ian Dempsey—A former member of the covert ops team Prospero, Ian has tracked down the next piece of the puzzle to find missing Prospero member Jack Coburn. Just his luck, the clue brings Ian face-to-face with his wife, and the distraction just might get them both killed.

Hans Birnbacher—A German tourist on Meg's hike, Hans asks too many questions to be an innocent bystander.

Sheriff Pete Cahill—The sheriff has a thing for Meg and isn't too pleased to see her husband show up. Will his anger jeopardize Ian's investigation?

Matt Hudson—Meg's boss isn't much of a businessman, but would he make a deal with terrorists to save his company?

Travis Dempsey—Meg's son meets his father for the first time and Ian has to face his fears about fatherhood, which are put to the ultimate test.

Kayla Shepherd—A CIA operative who risks her life to find Jack Coburn.

Farouk—Prospero's former nemesis has expanded his business model and taken his terror worldwide, and this time it's personal.

Colonel Scripps—Prospero's coordinator, the colonel knows he can summon all the former team members with one call. He just hopes it's not too late to save Prospero's leader, Jack Coburn.

Jack Coburn—The former leader of Prospero and current hostage negotiator has run into a little trouble. Can he depend on his brothers in arms to save him, or is he going to have to save himself?

Prologue

He crouched beside the edge of the outcropping that had saved his life and peered at the trail snaking below him toward the small village at the base of the mountain. He narrowed his eyes and assessed the terrain—rugged but doable. He had to get to that town if it killed him. And it just might.

He flattened his belly against the rough slab of rock, scooted toward the edge and swung his legs over the side, sliding the rest of his body into oblivion. He hung onto the ledge with calloused hands, his legs swinging freely beneath him, the sharp pain in his ribs almost cutting off his breath. He fumbled against the side of the cliff with the toe of his boot until it met the foothold he'd scoped out minutes before.

Bracing all of his weight on the meager indentation in the side of the mountain, he released his grip on the edge of the outcropping and did a freefall before clutching at some scrubby bushes for support.

Okay, off his stone savior and pinned to the side of a hostile cliff.

The rough-and-tumble trail below him beckoned, and he extended his long frame, searching for the next foothold. He could do this. Somehow he knew he'd done it before—maybe not this particular cliff, maybe not this particular trail—but his hands and feet moved with a natural rhythm down the face of the mountain.

His head throbbed and he could feel his scalp prickle as the knot on the back of his skull grew bigger and harder. As if to remind him he had other injuries to worry about, a trickle of blood crawled down his cheek and he flicked it away with his tongue—blood, sweat and dirt creating a nauseating taste in his mouth.

He glanced over his shoulder, tempted to release his hold and drop to solid earth, but his aching body couldn't absorb another fall. He continued his scrappy descent, blocking out the protesting screams and wails from the various cuts, scrapes and bruises dotting him from head to toe.

Two feet above terra firma, he dropped to the ground, his heavy boots cushioning the impact. As he hit the dirt and gravel feetfirst, he crouched down and folded his body forward, almost touching his forehead to the ground.

The rising sun warmed his back, and he rolled his shoulders to spread its heat through his stiff torso. He jerked his head up at the tinkling sound of a bell and gazed at the village hugging the bottom of the mountain.

Licking his lips, he pushed to his feet. He squeezed his eyes shut briefly against the pain that shot through his skull. Then he put one foot in front of the other as he trod down the trail toward civilization. He hoped to God someone down there could tell him how the hell he'd awakened on an outcropping in the middle of a mountain range.

Oh, and it would be a big plus if someone could tell him his name.

Chapter One

Meg O'Reilly's heart slammed against the wall of her chest. And it had nothing to do with the altitude.

A tall, athletic man hopped off the Rocky Mountain Adventures van and Meg gulped, feeling like one of those cartoon characters with the googly eyes. The drop-dead gorgeous tourist with the short brown hair and drool-worthy body ignored her—and her googly eyes—while he helped a blonde adjust a backpack.

But she hadn't missed the dark brows shooting up to his hairline when he'd caught sight of her. Meg clung on to the strap of her own backpack, hitched over one shoulder, and scanned the group for a hidden camera or some reality TV host jumping from behind a tree and screaming, "You've been punked!"

Gabe, the driver of the van, hopped from the last step and swept his arm in Meg's direction. "This is Meg O'Reilly, your hiking guide. If you feed her chocolate chip cookies, she might tell you about her adventures climbing Mount Everest."

Impressed murmurs merged with the roaring in Meg's ears, but she pasted a smile on her face anyway, and with a trembling hand waved to the assembled group. Tall, dark and handsome broke away from the pack, striding forward, extending his large, gloved hand.

"Good to meet you, Meg. I'm John Shepherd, and this is my wife, Kayla." He jerked his left thumb over his shoulder toward the smiling blonde as he gripped Meg's hand in a clasp strong enough to snap her bones.

Meg narrowed her eyes and squeezed back. She knew darned well Ian, or rather John Shepherd, or whatever he was calling himself these days, wasn't married to some buxom blonde.

He was still married to her.

"Welcome to the tour…John. This is a rugged hike. Are you sure you're up to it?" She scanned the muscular frame that made her question ludicrous, before allowing her gaze to meander back to his face. Then she turned up her lips in a false, sweet smile.

He flashed an answering grin, his broad shoulders relaxing. Why the tension? He must've known she wouldn't blow his cover. Hadn't she always been the dutiful little spy's wife?

Until the end.

"I think I can handle it, even though I've never attempted Everest. That must've been some experience."

Ian should know. They had met on her first and only Everest expedition. Formed an alliance on that mountain. Had each other's backs. Fell in love.

Swallowing the annoying lump in her throat, Megan brushed past Ian and greeted the rest of her group— several couples, a single man from Germany, a mother-daughter duo and a trio of women celebrating a fortieth birthday. They all looked fit and ready for the arduous twelve-mile hike up to the top of the mountain, including Ian's "wife" Kayla.

As Meg explained the rules of the hike to her group, she stole a few glances at Kayla, assessing the fresh-faced, sturdy woman in red fleece. She had to be Ian's fellow agent in Prospero, the undercover ops group that had consumed Ian's life during their two short years of marriage.

The question remained. What the hell were they doing on her hike?

"Are there any questions?" *Besides her own.* Meg hooked the left strap of her backpack over her shoulder and snapped the catch in the front. She answered a few questions about photo ops and first aid, thankful she could recite the answers in her sleep, since Ian's presence on the hike had her brain in a fog.

"We travel twelve miles to the top and take the train back down. Stay on the trail and drink plenty of water, even though it feels cold. We'll make several photo stops, so keep your cameras ready for some awesome pictures of waterfalls and gorges."

While the hikers drank some water and stamped their feet against the cold ground, Meg turned on her radio and slipped it into the pocket of her down vest. Wedging a shoulder against the door of the van, she said to Gabe, "Are you going straight back to the office?"

"Yeah." He started the van's engine. "I'm making another pickup there for Jason's hike to Cascade Falls."

"Make sure the radio's on at the office." Meg tipped her head back and surveyed the gray morning sky. "I don't think it's supposed to snow yet, but we'll probably get an afternoon thundershower or two, and you never know this time of year."

Gabe rubbed his gloved hands over the steering wheel, huffing out a cold breath. "Call Scott if you need help. He's out on the trails today. But it looks like you have a good group here. I even had them singing on the van."

Meg rolled her eyes. "You would. But singing isn't

going to keep them safe on a muddy trail with a ten-thousand-foot drop."

"Singing won't, but you will. You haven't lost one yet, Meggie."

Meg snorted and smacked the door after Gabe cranked it shut. Then she spun around to face Ian and the rest of her group.

Since Ian excelled at keeping secrets, she'd probably never find out what he and his partner were doing here. Of course, Meg had been keeping the biggest secret of all, and since she had no intention of revealing her secret to Ian, she didn't expect him to fill her in on the reason for his appearance on one of her hikes.

She knew it didn't have anything to do with her. He'd been as surprised to see her here as she'd been to see him…with a wife in tow.

Once everyone had stashed their water bottles and secured their packs, Meg moved to the front of the group and led them to the trailhead. She turned and they gathered around her in a semicircle of expectant faces.

"At the base of the trail we have a little room to spread out, but on some parts of the trail, especially at the higher elevations, we'll have to walk single file." She held out her hands, palm up. "We might get some rain, so I hope you all brought some rain gear or ponchos. If not, I have a few plastic ponchos in my pack."

The group fell in behind Meg as she tromped up the trail. The fallen leaves from the aspens crunched beneath her hiking boots and she inhaled their earthy, balsamic scent. She refused to allow Ian's surprise appearance to spoil one of her favorite hikes. She hadn't heard from the man once since their separation three years ago. Not that she didn't think about him every day of the week.

How could she help it, when each day their son,

Travis, looked at her through his father's green eyes flecked with gold?

Meg took a shuddering breath before stopping next to a clump of aspen. What would Ian do if he found out he had a two-year-old son? Probably shrug it off and return to some God-forsaken part of the globe to protect the citizens of the world. He'd made it clear during their marriage, and after the miscarriage of her first pregnancy, that he didn't want a family.

Crouching down, Meg scooped up a few pieces of bark and handed them around as she talked about the trees along the first leg of their trail. Ian and Kayla peered at a strip of bark, but Meg knew Ian's mind was churning, hatching plots and plans. His body almost vibrated with a restless energy—an energy she'd found irresistible when they first met.

The hikers traversed the first mile of the trail, falling into a rhythm and predictability. Several forged ahead of her and others hung back, slowing the group's progress. She wouldn't call them the easiest bunch she'd ever led, but then maybe she could blame Ian's presence for her irritability and impatience.

The German tourist kept close to Meg, peppering her with numerous questions in his slightly accented English. One of the couples dawdled, more interested in each other than the hike—probably newlyweds. Meg tried to suppress her envy. That's how it had been for her and Ian on Everest. The magnificent scenery could barely compete with their fascination with each other.

Two of the three women in the birthday group kept prodding their companion, who complained loudly about spending her vacation traipsing through a high elevation forest, instead of sitting in front of a bar after an afternoon massage.

Meg nudged the complainer in the side. "You'll get back in time for a massage, and there are plenty of bars over in Colorado Springs to keep you busy later. And with an air force base, and air force academy, there are lots of military guys in those bars if you like a man in uniform."

The woman growled, making claws with her fingers, and her friends giggled.

Maybe Ian's mission had something to do with the Schriever Air Force Base, although another guy in the Prospero unit, Buzz Richardson, was air force, while Ian handled mountain rescue. Was Ian trying to rescue something or someone in these mountains?

Not her problem.

Meg slid her backpack off one shoulder. "Let's stop here and take a break, get some water. There are some beautiful views of the waterfall from the lookout point. We'll be hiking to a platform about midway to the top of those falls, for a closer view."

A few of the hikers staked out some boulders, collapsing on top and chugging their water. Several dropped their packs and wandered to the edge of the trail for a better look at the falls in the distance. The honeymooners massaged each other's shoulders.

As Meg unhooked her canteen from her pack, Ian sidled up next to her. "Meg, I wanted to ask you about some purple flowers we saw back on the trail. I can point them out to you."

Meg choked on her water and it dribbled down her chin. She'd have never made it in her sister's circle, even if she'd wanted that lifestyle. "Describe the flower to me and I'll tell you all about it."

"I'd rather show you. They're not far, and I don't see any like them in this spot." Ian raised his brows, probably incredulous, she wasn't jumping at the chance to discover his mission.

She wanted to tell him to go to hell, but her curiosity trumped her petty need to strike out. "Okay, but I don't want to leave the group for too long. We need to get moving if we're going to meet the afternoon train at the top."

Nodding, Ian tromped ahead, effortlessly traversing the rugged trail, while the other hikers remained sprawled out behind them, still panting from the morning's exertion. If he knew the terrain, Ian could lead this hike in her place.

If he knew the terrain.

As soon as they rounded the first bend, he grabbed Meg's arm. "Thanks for not blowing our cover. I had no idea you were leading this hike. The website listed some guy, Richard."

Ian hadn't planned on seeing her at all. She gulped. "Richard got sick. I took his place."

"Can't pretend I'm happy about it, but I told Kayla we could count on you."

Even through Meg's multiple layers and Ian's gloves, his touch felt like a brand on her arm. She shrugged him off. "I'm guessing her real name isn't Kayla."

Ian lifted a shoulder. "I figured you'd catch on."

"And I figured my ex-husband wouldn't choose one of my hikes as an opportunity to relive old times."

"Husband."

"What?"

"I'm your husband."

Meg stumbled back, Ian's words punching her in the gut. The aching pit of emptiness she felt at his words surprised her. Ending her marriage to Ian had broken her heart, but she thought she'd finally recovered. She'd even accepted most of the blame, since she was the one who had changed the rules of their relationship. Seeing him again, and the way his grin tilted up on one side, contrasting with the sharp intensity of his eyes, carved open a hollow space in her heart—one she thought she'd filled ages ago.

One she'd better start filling with something. Anger would do.

She dug her boots into the dirt and squared her shoulders. "What are you and your partner doing on this hike?"

His grin vanished, a furrow forming between his brows. "You know I can't tell you that, Meg."

"Blah, blah, blah. Same old crap with you, Dempsey. You're obviously using Rocky Mountain Adventures for some reason, or you'd hike in here on your own. Why didn't you just call and ask me? Why'd you have to sneak in here pretending to be a tourist...*John?*"

He put his finger to his lips. "Not so loud."

"What if I blew your cover, right here, right now?" She narrowed her eyes at the way his jaw tightened. "I'd be jeopardizing national security or something like that, wouldn't I?"

"Not only national security, but your own and that of every tourist on this hike." He cocked his head. "Why so angry, Meg? You're the one who ended it, although you never did bother filing for divorce."

Her cheeks burned and she lifted her face to the cool air. "You couldn't handle a real relationship, one with trust and commitment."

"That's bull. I committed to you with everything I had. I love...loved you with everything I had. When you lost the baby..."

"A baby you didn't want."

"I could've grown used to the idea."

Meg snorted. "That's big of you."

He grabbed her shoulders. "I'm not playing the pity card, but you know damn well why the thought of a child scared the hell out of me."

"You're not your father, Ian. You never were." Her eyes burned with tears as frustration gnawed at her insides. She should've been able to make him see that. She'd failed him.

His grip on her shoulders softened to a caress. "You made me see that more than anyone, Meg."

She swayed toward him, and then clenched her hands into fists. She couldn't take this trip with him again, especially while he was in the middle of one of his covert operations, shutting her out, keeping secrets.

She stuffed down her guilt over keeping Travis from him. He'd probably rather not know about his son.

Whatever Ian and Kayla decided to do once the hike ended didn't concern her. She'd deliver them to the top of the mountain, along with the rest of the tourists, and they could knock themselves out with their secret agent crap. Then maybe she'd get that divorce she'd been putting off, and then maybe she'd better tell him about his son.

"Where's the purple flower?"

Ian's nostrils flared for a second and then he grinned. He dropped his hands from her shoulders and swooped down, plucking a flower from the ground. Cradling the small flower in his palm, he said, "Here it is."

"It's poisonous."

He tipped his hand over and the flower floated to the dirt. Meg crushed the petals beneath her boot as she headed back up the trail to the other hikers.

Perched on a boulder, Kayla raised her head from her

small guide book and her brows shot up. She didn't know her partner very well, if she thought Ian had spilled the beans about their mission.

Meg adjusted her pack. "Our next stop will be the viewing deck for the falls, but on the way keep your eye out for some small mountain critters—picas, squirrels and some cute rodents."

Meg did a head count and frowned. "Where's…" She snapped her fingers, "Russ and Jeanine?"

The lovey-dovey couple emerged from some under-brush, holding hands. Wide-eyed, Jeanine asked, "Are you waiting for us?"

A few of the other hikers smirked while Meg nodded, clenching her teeth against her irritation, recognizing it for what it was—jealousy. "Okay, everyone's accounted for. Let's go."

The furtive conversation with Ian had rattled her. He hadn't been expecting to see her leading this hike, but he obviously knew she worked as a guide for Rocky Mountain Adventures.

Had he been keeping tabs on her? Not likely. He'd given no indication he knew she had a child. His child.

AN HOUR LATER, Meg halted at the top of the fifty-three wooden steps that descended to the viewing platform for the waterfall. "If you don't want to expend your energy climbing down and then back up these steps, you're welcome to wait here. We still have another two hours of hiking ahead of us."

A few groans met this statement and Meg grinned. *Wussies.*

She trudged down the steps with the heartier members of the group, steering clear of Ian and Kayla, who branched out in different directions. After pointing out a few features of the falls and the river running through the canyon, Meg climbed back up the stairs and took some questions while waiting for the others.

As Meg opened her mouth to answer yet another question, a scream echoed through the canyon where the waterfall plunged into jagged rocks. The sound sent a shot of cold dread straight to Meg's heart.

Her gaze darted among the hikers gathered on the trail, their mouths agape. Who was missing from the group? She noted the absence of Ian immediately, along with his pretend wife, two other couples, and the German tourist.

God, please don't let it be Ian.

"Wait here." Meg charged through the group and headed toward the steep stairs leading to the viewing platform of the falls. Her hiking boots clumped down each wooden step, the blood thrumming through her veins. Like a herd of cattle, the hiking group thundered down the steps behind her.

The ease with which they ignored her instruction didn't surprise her. They were a difficult bunch, and that didn't even take into account the appearance of Ian on the tour with a make-believe wife.

As Meg rounded the last bend of the staircase, she froze, her foot hanging off the bottom step. The splintered wood of the broken railing that separated the lookout deck from the rugged mountain terrain resembled sharp teeth. Meg swallowed and held her hand out behind her. "Stop."

She didn't need anyone else going over…if that's what had happened.

Meg crept up to the gaping rail and held on to a solid piece of wood as she crouched down. The white water swirled beneath her and a slash of red bobbed near an outcropping of rocks.

Red fleece.

A hand gripped her shoulder, and she twisted around to look into Ian's stormy green eyes.

"I—I think it's Kayla. Is she missing? What about the others?"

Ian's hold tightened, his fingers pinching into her flesh through her layers. "It's Kayla."

"Oh my God, Ian. I'm so sorry." She clapped her hand over her mouth. She'd called him by his real name and not the alias, John Shepherd, he'd been using on the hike.

No wonder he'd never trusted her with any of his secrets.

Within seconds, the rest of the hikers crowded behind them, gasping and crying out. They'd expect Ian to be wild with grief with his wife lying fifty feet below, snagged on the wicked rocks that tumbled along the riverbank. Meg knew more than grief would assault Ian at the possible death of his partner.

He suppressed those emotions behind his tight expression as he peered at Kayla's still form below them. Then he covered his face with one hand.

"I'll call for help." Meg plucked the radio out of her pocket and slid into the familiar mode of enlisting Ian's leadership skills. "If you can stay with the other hikers, I'll attempt to climb down in case…in case she survived the fall. There's never been an accident here before."

As the others murmured and sobbed, Ian lifted his head and brushed Meg's ear with his lips.

"This was no accident."

Chapter Two

Meg's skin blanched beneath her freckles. This was why he'd kept his business to himself when they'd been together. He'd never wanted to scare her or make her feel any fear.

Or put her life in jeopardy.

But, for her own safety, he had to make it clear that one of her tourists had just shoved Kayla through the wooden railing. Had Kayla's attacker identified her as CIA, or just pegged her as a nosy tourist who'd stumbled onto something she shouldn't have?

Ian covered his face with his hands and hunched his shoulders. He rocked forward, moaning Kayla's name. Twisting his head to the side, he peered at the hikers between his fingers.

If the killer ID'd Kayla as an agent, he had to know Kayla's so-called husband was part of the team. Which one of the shocked faces masked a killer?

Meg's radio crackled as she reported the incident, her voice strong and steady. Whatever Meg felt right now, she'd do her job.

She turned toward him, her blue eyes wide. "They can't send in a helicopter—too dangerous with the falls so close—but the El Paso County Search and Rescue is going to hike in and move her downstream. The sheriff's department is sending in a helicopter to airlift her from that area."

Ian shrugged off his pack. "I'm not waiting for some search-and-rescue team to get here. She might be alive."

And if Kayla still had breath in her body, she'd identify her attacker.

"I can't let you do that." Probably wondering how far she had to carry the charade, Meg shifted her gaze beyond him to the group of shocked tourists, and Ian followed her line of sight.

The birthday girls huddled together whispering, while the honeymooning couple, stumbling on the scene late, clung to each other, faces white. The German tourist… snapped photos.

A burst of anger exploded behind his eyes, but Ian took a deep breath. He had to get down to Kayla. Meg knew he was just as capable of hiking down to Kayla and moving her body downstream as the volunteer search-and-rescue team on its way. More capable, since he'd been a member of the army's mountain division before joining the covert ops team, Prospero.

Ian decided to make it easy for her. He raised his voice, a sob cracking his words. "That's my wife down there. You can't stop me."

He launched over the side of the deck, his boots fitting into the footholds he'd scoped out minutes earlier. As he scaled down the rocky cliff side, he heard voices above him. Several minutes later, a shower of pebbles rained down on his head. He glanced up to see Meg following his path down the side of the cliff.

He tilted his head back and called to her, "Shouldn't you be keeping an eye on your group?" Although, in all honesty, he'd rather have Meg down here with him than up there with a possible killer.

She responded in a tinny voice. "One of our guys in the area heard the radio call and just showed up. He's going to get the group to the top."

For the next several minutes Ian heard only his own heavy breathing and the roar from the waterfall. Meg, following his path, made a steady descent in his wake, occasionally dislodging pebbles that pelted his head and hands.

Reaching the bottom of the craggy cliff face, Ian jumped to the ground, his boots splashing in the river where it tumbled over slick rocks. He reached Kayla in two strides and crouched beside her lifeless form. Her blond hair floated in the water, and her eyes stared, unseeing, at the falls.

Ian checked her pulse. Nothing. He hadn't known Kayla well, but she'd shown a fierce loyalty to Jack Coburn. She'd volunteered for this mission as soon as she found out about Jack's disappearance. And she'd done so without the approval or knowledge of her employer, the CIA.

There'd be hell to pay for this screwup.

Meg panted over his shoulder. "Is she...?"

"She's dead." Ian passed his hand over Kayla's eyes, closing them to the world for the last time.

Meg grasped his shoulder for support as she choked. "Who did this?"

"One of your so-called tourists." He pointed his index finger toward the top of the cliff.

"Do you think Scott will be safe?"

"Scott?"

"The other guide who's finishing the hike for me."

"He'll be fine as long as he doesn't start asking

questions. And why should he? But I'll need a list of all the people on the hike." The colonel had misjudged the enemy. He thought the terrorist scum would sneak in here in the dead of night to recover their lost property. Instead, someone had posed as a tourist, hitting on the same plan as Ian.

With deadly results.

"Why are you so sure Kayla was pushed? Maybe she fell." Meg kneeled on the ground and felt for a pulse in Kayla's neck.

"You told me yourself, nobody has ever had an accident on that trail. Kayla falling from the platform is too coincidental. She and I are on this hike looking for... something, and she winds up dead at the bottom of a cliff."

"Do you think she found that something?"

"If not, she must've been getting warm."

Meg's radio crackled, and she informed her home office that she and the victim's husband were with the body and that Scott was leading the rest of the group to the top of the mountain.

She ended the transmission and pocketed the radio. "Did you hear that? They want us to wait with Kayla until search and rescue gets here."

"I can move her downstream to wait for the helicopter. The El Paso County Search and Rescue doesn't have to waste its time hiking down here."

"And blow your cover? Remember, you're a tourist who just lost his wife."

And an agent who just lost his partner.

Ian sank down on the nearest boulder and buried his face in his hands—for real this time. He'd wanted to go on this operation alone, but the colonel thought he'd be less suspicious as part of a couple. That didn't work out too well. He plowed his fingers through his hair and cursed.

The pressure of Meg's hand rubbing circles on his back calmed him. He squeezed his eyes shut and allowed the warmth to seep through his body. God, he'd missed her touch these past three years.

Why had he let Meg go without a fight? *Because she deserved better.* A better husband than one who'd been halfway across the world when his wife suffered a miscarriage. He blamed himself. His mission had caused her too much stress. His secrets had strained the trust between them.

Truth was he had no idea how to be a good husband and even less of an idea how to be a good father. His role model had been neither.

Apparently, he also sucked at being a good partner.

His muscles tensed, and the pressure of Meg's hands increased. "I'm sorry about Kayla, but it's not your fault, Ian. If she was an agent with Prospero, she knew the risks."

Ian twisted around to look into Meg's clear blue eyes. Did she really know so little about Prospero, the military covert ops team that worked so deep undercover, sometimes their own government didn't know what they were doing?

What did he expect? He'd compartmentalized that entire side of his life, keeping Meg so far away from it that she'd felt abandoned by him and excluded from the closeness he'd shared with the members of that group.

He dragged in a deep breath of crisp mountain air. "Kayla wasn't part of Prospero, Meg. She joined our mission from the CIA. There is no Prospero anymore. We disbanded almost two years ago."

She pushed up abruptly. "Th-then what are you doing here? Are you working for the CIA now?"

"Not exactly." He rubbed his knuckles across his jaw. What the hell. They were alone and he owed her big time. Through no fault of her own, she was smack in the middle of this thing, and she had a right to know why he and Kayla, and apparently some terrorist, had commandeered her hike on a fresh fall morning.

"Sit down. We can't do anything for Kayla now anyway, except wait for search and rescue to move her body." He patted a space beside him on the rough boulder.

She perched next to him, looking poised for flight, her back stiff, her eyes wary.

"Do you remember Jack Coburn from Prospero?"

She nodded and her silky strawberry-blond ponytail bobbed behind her. "I remember all the guys from Prospero—the colonel, Jack, Riley and Buzz. You were all so close. You had some kind of unspoken bond, so thick it was a like a cord binding you all together."

Her voice sounded wistful, and Ian reached out and grabbed her hand. He should've been forging that bond with his wife, but those guys had been the closest thing he'd ever had to family. Until he'd met Meg.

"Jack went missing a few months ago." His own words punched him in the gut all over again, and he convulsively squeezed Meg's hand. "After Prospero disbanded, we all went our separate ways. Always the silver-tongued devil with nerves of steel, Jack took a job as a hostage negotiator."

"You mean like with the FBI?"

"No. Jack worked...*works* freelance. Large corporations, newspapers and private citizens hire him to rescue loved ones, usually being held hostage in foreign countries."

"That sounds dangerous."

"You don't know the half of it. Jack was working a case in Afghanistan when he disappeared off the face of the earth." Ian clenched his teeth. The CIA had labeled Jack a traitor, but the spooks in the Agency didn't know Jack. Except Kayla, Kayla knew Jack.

Meg ran a finger along his tight jaw. "So what are you doing in Colorado?"

"One of the other former Prospero members, Riley, traced Jack's disappearance to a drug cartel in Mexico, which in turn led to an arms dealer here in the States. The arms dealer's clients were transporting some kind of weapon in a private plane over this area. We had a line on the plane, and Buzz Richardson picked it up and forced the plane down at the air force base. Unfortunately for us, the weapon wasn't onboard."

Meg covered her mouth with her hand, her brows shooting up to her bangs. "What happened to it?"

Ian spread his arms wide. "Buzz thinks they jettisoned it right here, once they spotted him on their tail."

"A weapon here in Crestville? Why wasn't it on the news? How come there was no rescue operation?"

"This is all under the radar, Meg." He rubbed the pad of his thumb across her knuckles. "The pilot never filed a flight plan, had no instruments on board and had no radio contact with any towers. It's as if that airplane never existed…except on Buzz's personal radar."

"How did Buzz figure out the occupants of the plane ditched their cargo here?"

"He did a little creative interviewing of the folks on that plane. One couldn't take the pressure and cracked, admitting they'd tossed the suitcase overboard."

"What's in that case, Ian?" Meg clamped her lower lip between her teeth, her eyes round and definitely worried.

He lifted one shoulder, hoping she'd believe him. "We don't know. Whatever's in that case came from an arms dealer named Slovenka. We know it's a weapon of some sort. A very expensive weapon. A very dangerous weapon."

"Didn't Buzz's creative questioning unearth the type of weapon?"

"Uh, the suspect killed himself before he gave away anything more." Damn, he hated exposing her to this stuff.

Meg hugged herself and said, "And now the rest of them are back trying to find the weapon…along with you. Do you think the arms dealers are after it, or the terrorists they sold it to?"

He didn't want her involved, but that decision was beyond him. He eased out a long breath. "Slovenka got his money. The location of the weapon is now the purchasers' problem."

She snapped her fingers, getting into the spirit of the thing. "The German tourist—he lingered behind to take pictures. Maybe Kayla saw something and he pushed her."

"A lot of them lingered behind. It could be any one of them, Meg. Just because the German traveled solo doesn't necessarily make him the prime suspect. Maybe it's one of the married couples with the same idea as Kayla and…"

Ian squeezed his eyes shut and pinched the bridge of his nose. This is one aspect of active duty Ian didn't miss—losing coworkers.

Meg entwined her fingers with his. "Did you know her well?"

He shook his head. "Not at all, not even her real name. It's better that way."

The whomping sound of helicopter blades cut off further conversation.

Shading her eyes, Meg pushed up from the boulder. "Search and rescue is here. The chopper will drop off the team and they'll hike upstream to retrieve Kayla."

Meg radioed the helicopter, giving the rescue team their exact location. Fifteen minutes later, two hikers emerged from the thick foliage.

As the men examined Kayla's body, Ian held his breath. He couldn't get into anything with them right now. He wanted to search the immediate area before anyone else had an opportunity to return.

One of the search-and-rescue members rose and patted Ian's shoulder. "I'm sorry for your loss, Mr. Shepherd. Was your wife leaning over the railing when she fell?"

Ian shook his head, squeezing his eyes shut. "I wasn't with her...and neither were any of the other hikers."

At least nobody on the hike claimed to have seen what occurred, but Ian knew at least one person, possibly two, knew exactly what had happened to Kayla.

The rescue team unfolded and secured a stretcher and lifted Kayla's body onto it. As they turned her, Kayla's camera dangled from her neck.

Ian's hand shot out. "Can I take her camera?"

"Sure." The search-and-rescue hiker carefully slipped the camera strap over Kayla's head and handed the camera to Ian. Then he turned to Meg. "Meg, once we load the stretcher onto the helicopter, there's room for only one more. We'll take Mr. Shepherd with us and you can hike back up."

"No!" Ian shouted the word, and three startled faces turned in his direction. Ian curled his hand over Kayla's cold fingers and slid the wedding band from her left hand. "M-my wife's wedding band is missing. I need to find it. I can't leave without that ring. Leave me here. I want to be alone."

Ian covered his face with his hands so he didn't have to do any more explaining. He felt Meg's hand on his arm. "It's okay, Greg. I'll hike back up with Mr. Shepherd. I'll make sure he gets to the top, and I'll arrange transportation for him to the hospital in Colorado Springs."

Through the spaces between his fingers Ian saw the rescue workers exchange a worried glance, but it didn't look like they wanted to argue with a bereaved, irrational spouse. He should've figured Meg would volunteer to stay behind with him.

Before the search-and-rescue team hiked back to the chopper with Kayla's body on the stretcher between them, Ian clutched Kayla's stiff fingers, kissed her cheek and whispered, "I'll tell Jack you sacrificed everything."

He and Meg watched the hikers disappear before turning back to the river and the falls. "You could've gone with the chopper."

"And leave you here alone?" Meg twisted her ponytail around her hand. "I'm going to be in big enough trouble as it is. I'll most likely be suspended from my job, if not fired, while Rocky Mountain Adventures waits for the phone call from your lawyer."

Ian smacked his fist against his palm. He hadn't thought of that. Any red-blooded, litigious American would sue Rocky Mountain Adventures in a heartbeat for this accident.

"Sorry Meg-o. I waltz back into your life after three years and look what happens."

She shrugged, her cheeks flushing a rosy pink at the nickname. "At least I know you don't have any intention of suing us."

Ian clicked the buttons on Kayla's wet digital camera. "If I'm lucky, Kayla snapped some photos of whatever she wasn't supposed to see, or maybe even got a couple of shots of her attacker."

Meg leaned over his shoulder, but the camera's screen remained black. Ian blew out a breath and dropped the camera, where it swung from his neck. "The water may have damaged it or maybe the battery's dead."

"You stayed behind to search this area, didn't you?"

"Of course, but I didn't plan to involve you."

"You never do."

Ouch.

Meg slid her backpack from her shoulders. "I have some binoculars. Maybe Kayla spotted something across the river or at the top of the falls."

Their gloved fingers met as Meg passed the binoculars to him, and for a moment the electricity crackled between them, even though their skin didn't even touch. Meg snatched her hand back, as if burned. *Yeah, she felt it, too.*

Ian had been on high alert from the moment he stepped off the van and discovered Meg was going to be their guide. He hadn't had a single opportunity to relish being close to her again. This reunion bore no resemblance to the one he'd played over and over in his head these past three years without her.

And the situation had gotten even worse.

"I'll have a look along the riverbank. Maybe Kayla spotted something in the water snagged on the rocks."

She put her hands on her hips. "Just what am I looking for anyway? What kind of suitcase is this?"

"Your guess is as good as mine. It's probably a hard-sided case, not too big, not too small." Ian trained the binoculars on the hillside across the canyon, scanning every ledge, every tree. He caught his breath a few times, only to be disappointed.

What had Kayla seen from that overlook to prompt someone to kill her on the spot?

Meg's radio crackled and a voice sputtered across the airwaves. "Meg? Meg, are you there?"

As Meg answered the radio call, Ian sharpened his focus to zero-in on an area behind the falls.

"I'm here with...Mr. Shepherd, Matt. We're on our way back, unless you can send another helicopter in to pick us up."

Ian cursed. The shiny object behind the wall of water had been a trick of the sunlight, now throwing shafts of light through the clouds. He hoped if the search-and-rescue team sent another chopper in, they'd take their time.

The radio hissed with static. "Not sure we can do that, Meg, but that's not why I called. There's another hiker missing from your group."

Ian spun around and dropped the binoculars, which banged against his chest.

Meg's eyes widened as she gripped the radio with two hands. "Someone's missing from the hike? Who?"

Ian's breath stopped as a red dot of light appeared between Meg's eyes. His gut clenched for one second before he soared through the air and tackled her.

Chapter Three

As Meg hit the ground, the radio flew out of her grasp. She opened her mouth to yell, but Ian clamped a hand across her lips.

"Shh." He shifted his weight on top of her, pushing the air out of her lungs and smashing her face into the moist dirt.

Wet sand from the riverbank flooded her mouth, settling between her teeth, and she sputtered. Ian couldn't have picked a more perfect way to remind her why she'd left him—his complete devotion to his career at her expense.

His warm breath tickled her ear as he covered her body with his large frame. He draped his thigh across her hip, protecting her, shielding her. He couldn't have picked a more perfect way to remind her how much it had hurt to leave him—his complete and utter protectiveness of her.

He whispered, "Stay still a few more minutes. I saw a red laser bead from a weapon on your forehead."

Meg bucked beneath him as if someone had shocked her with a cattle prod. Was Ian trying to finish her off?

Ian stroked her ponytail and then lifted his head. Taking a deep breath, Meg turned her face into the wet mulch, the smell of the damp leaves and earth invading her nostrils. Maybe if she buried her head in the dirt this would all go away. Except Ian. She didn't want Ian to go away—not yet anyway.

Straddling her thighs, Ian rose to a sitting position. He held his finger to his lips and scanned the area with the binoculars. He reached for the backpack he'd dropped when he'd taken her down and pulled out a weapon.

Meg gasped, although Ian's hiking accoutrements shouldn't come as a surprise to her. Her husband had always been armed and dangerous.

Gripping his gun, Ian rolled off her body. "Stay low. We're going to have to hike out of here beneath some heavy cover. Get on the radio and find out who's missing from the hike."

Meg rolled onto her stomach, pointing to the racing river. "My radio's downstream somewhere. Another good reason for the company to fire me."

"I suppose you didn't happen to catch a name before I…uh, knocked the radio out of your hand?"

"No, but if we see one of the tourists wandering around out here in the wilderness, it's a pretty good bet he's our man."

"Or woman."

She grabbed his arm and pulled him close to the base of the hill. "We'll be safer following this path, instead of traipsing along the banks of the river."

Ian ducked beneath a tree and chugged some water from his bottle. He wiped the rim on the sleeve of his jacket and offered it to Meg. "I was hoping to search the area while we're here."

"You can't do that with someone aiming red lasers at our heads." She gulped the water down her parched throat too quickly and coughed and sputtered.

"Are you okay?" Ian pounded her back.

She twirled around, holding out her hands. "I'm choking on water. I don't need CPR."

Ian rubbed his brow with the back of his hand, still encased in a thick glove. "Sorry. How long can we hike along the base of the mountain before heading up to the trail?"

"About an hour." Meg tipped her head toward the falls. "Once we get past the waterfall, we can take a path back to the trail that's not as exposed as this one."

"Keep your eyes open. We might see the case or something else incriminating down here."

She blew a piece of hair, which had escaped from her ponytail, out of her face. "You don't have to tell me to keep my eyes open, but I'll be watching out for guns and red beams instead of someone's luggage, even if that luggage is lethal."

"I wonder if we're close." Ian adjusted his backpack and squinted into the dense foliage across the river. "That guy back there must've had a good reason for trying to take us out."

"Oh no, you don't." Meg had seen that look on his face one too many times. She tugged on his arm, which responded like an unmovable granite rock. "You're not wandering around here with someone taking potshots at you."

Ian quirked one eyebrow at her. She'd seen that look before, too. In fact, she knew his facial expressions as well as her own, as well as her son's, which imitated his father's in a remarkable way.

"You really care about my well-being, Meg-o? A few years ago you would've been pushing me out there to explore to my heart's content."

She shook her head, her ponytail swinging vigorously

from side to side. "I just didn't want to live with you anymore. I didn't want you dead."

"That's a relief." He chucked her under the chin and then tramped ahead of her on the trail hugging the mountainside.

Despite the chilly air, her skin burned where he'd touched her with his gloved finger. No wonder she couldn't get any kind of relationship off the ground. This man still had a place under her skin, and in her heart.

Twigs and leaves snapped and crackled beneath her hiking boots, mimicking the general action of her mind. Maybe if she concentrated on Ian's mission here in Colorado, instead of analyzing his facial expressions, she'd stop thinking about him in *that way*. His work had irritated her when they were together, since it seemed as if he'd cared about it and the other Prospero members more than he cared about her. That old shame crept over her again, heating her cheeks at the childish thought.

At the end of one of their arguments, Ian would laugh and tell her that she should've married a banker if she wanted sure and steady. Then he'd grab her and kiss her all over until she'd surrender and admit that she didn't want a banker. Then they'd make love until she'd forgotten her anger completely, sometimes until she'd forgotten her own name.

Shaking her head, she patted her cheek with her gloved hand. *The mission. Concentrate on the mission.*

Ian glanced over his shoulder. "Are you okay? I'm not going too fast for you, am I?"

She snorted. "This is my terrain, remember? If you knew the area, you wouldn't have needed Rocky Mountain Adventures to lead you in."

"Kayla and I should've tried hiking in ourselves. Then

she might still be alive." He kicked at a rock in his way and it skittered into the bushes.

"You don't know that." She grabbed his belt loop beneath his jacket until he came to a stop in front of her. "I'm sorry about Kayla, but she took the risk and knew the possible consequences."

"I tried to talk her out of coming along." Ian shoved his hands into his pockets and nudged at a stone set in the ground with the toe of his hiking boot. "But she wanted to help Jack any way she could."

"He's the kind of guy who inspires fierce devotion. That I remember." Meg also remembered Jack's intensity, his dark eyes and black hair. Out of all the men on the Prospero team, Jack was the only one without a relationship. Riley had been married to that poor society girl who had died in the bombing of that hotel. Buzz actually managed a relationship with a woman, Raven, who worked with Prospero. And of course she and Ian had struggled through a couple of years of marriage.

Only Jack remained aloof, solo, as if he knew he had a limited time on earth and didn't want to disappoint a woman with his early departure. Like now. Meg wrapped her arms around her body and shivered.

"Are you sure you're okay?" Ian gripped her shoulders and squeezed, trying to infuse some of his palpable strength into her.

She hadn't always felt safe with Ian emotionally, but the man had a protective streak a mile wide and would risk anything to protect her physically. When they climbed Everest together, he'd rushed to her rescue several times, even when she hadn't needed his help. Later he admitted he used the whole protective scenario as a ruse to get close to her.

He told her that, and her heart had melted in the

middle of a waist-high snowdrift at base camp. Nobody had ever come to her rescue before. She'd always been the strong, resilient type.

She had to be.

"I'm fine." She lifted her shoulders. "I was just thinking about Jack. Nobody has heard anything from him since he took that hostage negotiation job in Afghanistan?"

"Right." Ian dropped his hands from her shoulders and passed a hand across his mouth. "The last time I talked to him, I didn't even know he was going on assignment. He'd just gotten back from Colombia."

"What drives him?"

Ian shrugged. "The same thing that drove most of us in Prospero. A need to protect. A desire for justice." He grinned. "The thrill of an adventure."

"Yeah, you've got that last one covered."

"So do you, Meg." He cocked his head. "You could have had some cushy job at Daddy's software company. Why are you out here in the wilderness, leading people up and down mountains?"

Rolling her eyes, she jabbed his solid chest with her index finger. "And now you sound just like him."

He clutched his chest and staggered back. "Comparing me to Patrick O'Reilly is a cruel blow. Are you two still at each other's throats?"

"As long as I'm still mucking around out here in the wilderness we are. I never could quite measure up..." Meg straightened her spine and stamped her feet against the wet ground. "We'd better get moving."

Ian pushed off the rock, grabbed her by the waist and swung her in front of him on the trail. "You lead for a while."

Long after Ian dropped his hands, Meg felt his touch

burning through her multiple layers of clothing. She'd figured, after a few years apart, her automatic responses to the man would've died out. *No such luck.*

She sucked in her lower lip as she trudged along the trail, Ian breathing heavily behind her. She'd have to tell him about Travis. She'd always planned on it, but she'd had a hard time contacting Ian over the years.

Both of his parents had died even before she and Ian had gotten married, not that she'd missed any familial bonding. His parents had been druggies and alcoholics, a couple of losers who'd given up their son years ago. When they'd discovered Ian had made something of himself, they insinuated themselves back into his life. That hadn't lasted long. Even Ian's strong desire to reconnect with a mom and dad, any mom and dad, couldn't override his feelings of disgust for his parents.

Of course, Meg had to deal with the fallout from that experimental family reunion—a husband who never wanted to have children, a husband determined not to repeat the mistakes of his own father.

As if strong, capable, honorable Ian Dempsey remotely resembled his drunken father.

Ian touched her shoulder. "Is that where we hike up?"

She nodded at the direction of his pointing finger. "Yeah, we can scale up the side. It's a gentle slope with plenty of footholds."

Gripping the straps of his backpack, Ian scanned the gorge, his jaw tight. "I didn't see anything that could've led to Kayla's murder."

"Maybe it was just an accident." She touched his hand, wanting to give comfort as she'd tried to so many times during their marriage.

"That would be too much of a coincidence."

"Coincidences happen." Like her leading this hike instead of Richard. Maybe this coincidence was a sign that she needed to tell Ian about his son. This coincidence had dropped her husband into her lap—no excuses this time.

Ian chewed on his lower lip and narrowed his eyes. "Yeah, it's a coincidence that one of Prospero's old foes is involved in this deal, too."

"What do you mean?" Prospero had so many foes, she didn't think Ian could distinguish one from another.

"Prospero crossed swords with a particular mercenary terrorist several times. I swear, this gang seemed more interested in the money than any higher calling or cause. The leader of the cell, a guy named Farouk, had a hand in securing the money for this arms deal."

"Sounds like Farouk's broadening his horizons and traveling the world." Meg shrugged and then jerked her chin toward the vertical trail to their right. "Here's where we ascend."

Meg's hands found their way to the first holds, and her feet followed as if on autopilot. She cranked her head over her shoulder. "Just follow my path."

"I'm right behind you."

Meg reached the top and hauled herself over the edge, inching forward on her belly to make room for Ian. She rolled onto her back, propped up by her pack, and stared at the gray clouds ringing the peaks.

Whether or not Ian wanted to be involved in Travis's life, Meg resolved to tell him about his son before he ran off again in pursuit of bad guys, in his endless quest to save the world to make up for his parents' detachment from it.

Ian clambered over the edge and crouched on his haunches beside her. "Are you taking a nap, or what?"

Closing her eyes, Meg said, "Just waiting for the slow guy."

"There's one in every group." He tapped her on the shoulder and she opened one eye. "Are you ready?"

"I'm ready, but with a caveat."

"Uh-oh. Like I have to carry you the rest of the way?"

She snorted. "When have you ever had to do that?"

"Everest…not that you allowed me to carry you. You never ask for help, even when you need it."

Meg jumped to her feet, ignoring Ian's outstretched hand. Asking for help showed weakness—and gave the *askee* all sorts of power over you. "Well, here's the warning, and I guess you can call it asking for help. You need to give Rocky Mountain Adventures and maybe even the cops a heads-up as to your purpose out here. Your behavior at the death of your wife is going to seem really odd if you don't, and they're not going to expect you to hang around here once her body is sent home."

"That's an easy request." Ian yanked off his gloves and stuffed them into his pockets. "I was planning on giving them some info, but not all. Is that okay with you?"

"That'll work." She pointed to the trail ahead of them. "I think we'll be safer up here."

"You're probably right, but I'd rather be down there searching. If someone's shooting at us, chances are good he hasn't found the cargo either."

"You're going back down there, aren't you?" Ian never gave up when he really wanted something. That's how she knew he didn't really want her. He'd given up way too easily.

"In time. I owe it to Jack, and now I owe it to Kayla."

Meg sighed, not even bothering to argue. As they

negotiated the remainder of the trail, Ian regaled her with stories of his Everest adventures…without her. Apparently he'd been working as a guide since he left Prospero. She'd never gone back to Everest. She'd accepted her time on the mountain as a once-in-a-lifetime event, a goal to achieve and check off her list.

"But nothing beat the first time." He nudged her shoulder with his as they now walked side by side on the widened trail, which was fast coming to an end. "How come you never went back? I half expected to find you up there one day."

Could she blurt out the truth to him right here and now? How she couldn't go back to Everest because she had a greater purpose in life—the care and feeding of their son. She drew a deep breath of clear mountain air into her lungs and blew it out slowly.

They both jerked their heads up at the sound of yelling and cheering coming from the end of the trail. Several of her coworkers from Rocky Mountain Adventures were charging toward them.

Richard reached them first. He must've come in on his sick day. "My God, Meg, we were worried. What happened to your radio?"

"I lost it in the river. It's a long story, Richard."

Richard placed his hand on Ian's shoulder. "Mr. Shepherd, I'm sorry for your loss. Rocky Mountain Adventures will do everything in its power to launch an investigation."

"Thank you. Are the sheriff's deputies here yet? I need to talk to them."

"They're in the office."

Meg slid a glance toward Ian, now purposefully striding toward the A-framed building that housed the Rocky Mountain Adventures office at the top of the mountain.

"What about the other hiker? Before I lost radio contact, Matt said something about another hiker missing."

"He's still missing. German guy."

Ian's step faltered as he met Meg's gaze and lifted a brow. She could question Richard more thoroughly once they got to the office. Right now they had to clue in Matt that she hadn't lost one of her hikers through negligence, that a murderer, a terrorist, lurked in their midst.

They gathered in a circle in the office, everyone chattering at once. Matt came from the back and pulled Meg aside. "You had me worried when we lost contact. Also, I don't want to add to your stress level here, but you got a call when you were on the hike."

"A call?" Meg's heart hammered in her chest. Getting a call while on the job was never a good sign.

"It was Felicia. She had to take your son to the emergency room." Matt patted her arm. "It's nothing too serious. He fell off his tricycle and sliced his chin…got a few stitches."

Meg clutched the straps of her backpack as the blood rushed to her head in a quick succession of fear and relief. She stumbled back, her hip catching the edge of a bookshelf filled with pamphlets.

She put out a hand to steady herself and her gaze collided with a pair of icy green eyes drilling a hole into her very soul.

Looked like she didn't have to tell Ian about his son after all.

Chapter Four

Ian tried to assemble his jumbled thoughts, his breath coming out in short spurts. Had that man just mentioned Meg's *son?*

Meg was still clutching the edge of the magazine rack with white, stiff fingers. She dropped her gaze from Ian's, and turned to the man who had brought her the news, murmuring something in his ear.

Could that man be the father of Meg's son?

Hot, thick rage thudded against Ian's temples. Someone touched his shoulder and he spun around with clenched fists and nearly punched a face, any face.

"Mr. Shepherd?" A sheriff's deputy, his dark eyes dipping to Ian's battle-ready hands, raised a pair of eyebrows to the rim of his cowboy hat. "I'm Sheriff Cahill. I'm sorry for your loss. Can we speak in the back?"

Great. He'd almost assaulted an officer of the law, one who looked ready to accept the challenge. Probably some small-town sheriff with a chip on his shoulder...which was about to get bigger. Squeezing his eyes closed, Ian pinched the bridge of his nose. "I'm not Mr. Shepherd, but I'll explain all of that in a minute."

Cahill narrowed his eyes and scratched his jaw. "Something tells me I'm not going to like this...or you."

He glanced beyond Ian's shoulder. "Meg, you need to join us in the back room."

Ian shifted to the side of the irritated deputy to study Meg's face. She avoided his eyes and focused on Cahill's square jaw instead.

"I have a personal emergency, Pete." She held up a cell phone. "I'm going to make a call first."

Ian's brain had started functioning again and he realized the man, Matt, had referred to Meg's son as *your son*. Matt couldn't be the father. So who had that distinction? That lucky distinction.

Meg turned her back on him and put the phone to her ear. It didn't look like an explanation to him rated on her list of priorities right now. *Payback was a bitch.*

"We're set up in there." Cahill pointed a steady finger toward the corner of the room.

Ian trudged after the sheriff, feeling as if lead lined the bottom of his hiking boots. He wanted to listen in on Meg's conversation. Was she calling the boy's father?

The thought of Meg with another man tightened hot coils of anger in his belly. Then he let out a long breath. Although neither one of them had filed for divorce, Ian had no right to these possessive feelings about Meg. Had he really expected her to be as pristine as the snow frosting the top of the Rockies?

He hadn't thought about it. Didn't want to think about it.

Ian trudged into the room behind Cahill, and squared his shoulders as he faced the room with two other deputies seated at a serviceable table nicked with scratches and scars. Seamlessly, his thoughts shifted from Meg to the job at hand. Meg had resented his ability and propensity to switch his focus so quickly. But his work had always been a top priority for him. His parents had demonstrated to him what happened to people who couldn't commit to a job or responsibilities, and he refused to follow their example.

Cahill reached around Ian and snapped the door closed, the glass set in the center trembling with the force. "Okay now, Mr. Shepherd, or whoever you are, do you want to explain what's going on? Why did you stay behind and hike out of that canyon instead of boarding the chopper with your wife's body? And I don't want to hear about any wedding ring."

Ian reached into the inside pocket of his jacket and yanked out his wallet. He dug into one of the many compartments, his fingers closing around his I.D. Then he snapped it on the table top. "My name's Ian Dempsey, and I'm on a high-security mission for the United States military. The woman who…fell was my partner and CIA."

The three deputies sucked the air out of the room. That probably wasn't what they'd wanted to hear. And technically Ian hadn't told them the whole truth and nothing but. Colonel Scripps would vouch for him. He'd better, because the Agency didn't have any knowledge of this operation and would hang him out to dry.

"Dempsey?" Cahill cleared his throat. "What branch of the military are we talking about?"

His name seemed to stick in Cahill's gullet. Ian ran a finger along the inside collar of his jacket. He knew Cahill wouldn't be a pushover, by the set of his jaw and the suspicion in his eyes. "Intelligence. Covert ops."

Cahill cursed. "How much are you going to tell us and how much of that is going to come close to the truth?"

"My partner and I…" The door swung open and Ian snapped his mouth shut.

Meg poked her head into the room, her ponytail sliding over one shoulder. "Sorry."

"Everything okay with your little man, Meg?" Cahill's eyes softened to brown pudding when he looked at her. So she had that effect on the sheriff, too. All men wanted to be her Sir Galahad, but she preferred to don the armor herself. She'd learned from an early age that support came with a myriad of strings attached.

"How'd you know it was Travis?"

"Matt told me before all the craziness started. Is he okay?"

"He's fine. A cut beneath his chin and a few stitches." She folded her arms across her chest. "What did I miss?"

"Mr. Dempsey here was just telling us he's on a top-secret mission, and the poor lady who died wasn't his wife." Cahill wedged his hands on the table top and hunched forward. "How *did* your partner wind up at the bottom of the gorge, *Mr. Dempsey?*"

"I have no idea, *Deputy Cahill.*" Had Dempsey been the school bully who'd stolen Cahill's lunch money? The good sheriff seemed to sneer every time he said Ian's name.

Ian felt Meg's glance slide across his face, but he kept his gaze pinned to Cahill, as unpleasant as that was.

"Any chance you're going to tell me what you're doing in our neck of the woods?" The deputy's dark brows created a deep V over his nose.

If Ian ever did need help, he wouldn't hesitate to enlist Cahill's talents. Even though the sheriff clearly didn't like him, Ian knew he could trust the no-nonsense lawman. But he had no intention of putting the local law in some terrorist cell's line of fire.

Ian shrugged, raising the right corner of his lips. "I'm on a reconnaissance mission, Sheriff Cahill."

"I'm gonna need more than this two-bit badge to trust you, Dempsey." Cahill glanced at Meg and tapped the plastic CIA ID on the table, nudging it with his fingertip. "We have a woman's death in our jurisdiction."

Ian fumbled through his wallet to locate Colonel Scripps's latest cell phone number. The colonel wouldn't appreciate a call like Cahill's, but he'd come to expect being called upon to provide the legitimacy of his operatives from time to time.

At least he *had*. The members of Prospero hadn't been Colonel Scripps's operatives for a long time now, but the colonel was the one who had called them all out of retirement to help find Jack. He'd have to accept a few glitches along the way, especially since they were conducting operations stateside now, instead of in the lawless regions of Afghanistan or Somalia.

Cahill swept the card from the table and peered at it. Then he flicked it with his finger. "I'm off to do a little fact checking. Can you keep an eye on this one, Meg?"

Meg chewed her bottom lip as if seriously considering Cahill's question, or seriously considering something. "I—I can vouch for him, Pete. Ian Dempsey's my ex... my husband."

If Ian's earlier announcement about his true identity had floored the three deputies, Meg's knocked them out for the count. At least the other two deputies, whose mouths gaped like a couple of salmons swimming upstream. Cahill seemed to take the news in stride, pressing his lips into a thin line, a martial light gleaming in his dark eyes.

Leave it to Meg to put it all out there.

"Are you involved in this mess, Meg?" Cahill put a comforting hand on her shoulder and Ian felt like knocking it off.

She patted his long fingers. "No more than you are, Pete. Don't worry. Mr. Dempsey has everything under control."

Ian nearly choked on the snort he half swallowed. He had nothing under control, including his own emotions, but he wasn't about to correct Meg. Especially in front of this man who seemed way too close to his wife.

Cahill turned his cold gaze on Ian. "Watch yourself, Dempsey. Nobody walks into my town and plays fast and loose with Meg O'Reilly, husband or no husband."

"Furthest thing from my mind." Ian held up his hands, flexing his fingers so he wouldn't curl them into a fist.

When Cahill left the room, the other two deputies got down to business, asking about Kayla's accident. Although Ian had expressed his firm belief to Meg that Kayla's fall had been no accident, he backpedaled with the deputies. The last thing Ian or Prospero or Jack needed right now was a swarm of deputies blanketing the mountain looking for a weapon. Hell, Ian didn't even know what to look for at this point.

Meg kept her mouth shut through most of the questioning, not even raising an eyebrow at some of his blatant lies. She'd learned more as a spy's wife than he'd given her credit for.

As the deputies wound up their cross-examination, Ian had a couple of questions of his own. "Has anyone located the German tourist missing from the hike yet?"

Deputy Jensen scratched his chin and dropped his pencil on the pad of paper filled with Ian's lies and half truths. "As far as I know, he's still missing."

"How'd that happen, Brock? Matt was leading them

out, right?" Meg twisted her hands in front of her, lacing her fingers in an intricate pattern.

Did she still have her son on her mind? Ian wanted to sweep away all her worries. He'd always had that desire and had tried to keep his professional life out of their domestic life. It hadn't worked out as he'd planned. Meg had always felt shut out when all he'd wanted to do was protect her.

Jensen shrugged. "Apparently the guy kept hanging back and taking pictures, wandering off the trail. Matt was anxious to get the others up to the summit and eventually lost track of the guy."

"Just great." Meg rubbed her creased brow. "This is a banner day for Rocky Mountain Adventures, isn't it? The guy acted the same on our portion of the hike, but it could've been some kind of cover. Maybe he had something to do with Kayla's fall."

"Do you have his info from when he signed up for the hike?" Ian scraped his chair around to face Meg.

"I'm sure Matt's already looked him up, probably even called his hotel. I know his name was Hans, at least that's what he told me." She placed her palms flat on the table, as if to still their worried motion. "Do you think he's involved?"

"There's only one way to find out. We need to locate him and ask him a few pointed questions."

"We can at least help with that." Jensen drummed his fingers on the table in a staccato beat. "We'll search his hotel room and put a call out for his rental car, if he has one."

Ian nodded. "I appreciate that, Deputy Jensen."

The door burst open and Cahill huffed and puffed at the entrance to the office. "That Colonel Scripps is as closed-mouth as you are Dempsey, but you both check out. I mean, as far as I could check you out. Your background is a black hole."

Ian pushed back from the table. At least Cahill had removed the sneer from his voice when he'd mentioned his name. That had to be an improvement. "If you boys are finished here, I have to make some arrangements for Kayla, and I'm sure Meg has pressing business elsewhere."

God, he couldn't even bring himself to mention her son. Every thought of the boy punched him in the gut. They couldn't leave the subject hanging between them. She knew that he knew. He couldn't pretend otherwise... even if he wanted to. She'd deem him a coward if he avoided the topic.

Cahill held out the card with the colonel's number. "You can have this back, Dempsey. Just don't cause trouble in my town. I don't want any more unexplained dead bodies turning up, including yours."

"That's decent of you, Sheriff."

"Hell, that's not decent. Your corpse can turn up anywhere else, just not in Crestville."

Ian stuck out his hand. "I'll try my best to die outside of your jurisdiction."

Cahill squeezed his hand hard. "Appreciate it. Meg, do you need a ride to the emergency room, or is Travis home now?"

"Travis is still in the emergency room and I want to pick him up, but my car's at the office at the bottom of the mountain. Gabe can take me down in the van."

Cahill sliced a hand through the air. "By the time Gabe gets you down there, Travis will be home. I'll take you."

"I'll take her. I left my car up here and took the van down earlier, since we were skipping the train."

Two pairs of eyes, one dark the other bright blue, studied him. Heat suffused Ian's chest and he battled to keep it out of his face. A minute ago he couldn't stomach the thought of Meg with a child, someone else's child. Now he had a burning need to see him. He'd escaped torture by the enemy several times, and now he was prepared to inflict it on himself.

He held his breath, waiting for Meg's refusal. She had every right to keep him out of this part of her life, out of every part of her life. He'd let her go without a fight, and he'd regretted it every day of his sorry existence after he'd left. He had to pay some kind of penance now, a glimpse into what might have been between them. *Hell on earth.*

"Okay." Meg inclined her head, dropping her lashes. "You can give me a ride, Ian."

Ian swallowed. She seemed almost conciliatory, as if she owed him something. Would she tell him about the boy's father? Was he still in the picture? Did she want to rub his face in it?

Cahill tugged on Meg's ponytail. "We'll talk later. In the meantime, we'll keep our eye out for the missing hiker, although I'm sure Matt's already headed back to search for him."

Meg reached for the door and turned, pinning Ian with her gaze. "Don't you have to make arrangements for Kayla?"

"I'm sure Colonel Scripps has already started the wheels turning, since the good sheriff here informed him of the circumstances." Ian tapped his phone in his pocket. "I'll give him a call and we can work out the details on the way to the hospital."

Wrinkling her nose, Meg cocked her head. "Are you okay?"

No. He had a sour knot of regret gnawing at his insides for Kayla, and now this child that Meg shared with someone else. Someone worthy of fatherhood.

"It makes me sick to think about Kayla's family on the other end of this tragedy, but I'm determined to see this through." He bent his head to whisper in her ear. "For Kayla and Jack."

"If you need anything else, Pete, you know where to find me. And I'm leading another hike tomorrow."

Like hell she was. Ian wasn't going to allow that, not after what she'd been through today.

"And I gave my hotel to Deputy Jensen, so you know where to find me, too." Ian touched two fingers to his temple and swept Meg out the door.

They walked side by side in silence toward the parking lot, as drops of rain hit Ian's face and slid down his chin like chilly tears. Time to switch focus.

He and Meg had separated almost three years ago. She must've met someone else on the rebound. He'd had a couple of those relationships himself, but he'd recognized them for what they were—meaningless connections to fill the emptiness left by Meg. Definitely nothing serious enough to result in a child...a baby.

Meg's boy had to be a baby, less than two years old, unless she'd gotten pregnant immediately after their split. That had to be one, huge rebound.

Ian dug his keys out of his pocket and dropped them on the cold ground. *A tricycle accident.* He scooped up the keys with stiff fingers and hit the remote. The rental car beeped once as the locks popped and Ian opened Meg's door.

He walked around the back of the car, his steps slow. Babies didn't ride tricycles. How old did a kid have to be to master a trike? Two? Three?

His chest felt tight and he pounded on it and coughed. Damned altitude. Not like his body couldn't acclimate to heights, since he spent most of his time among the clouds. But he knew the altitude had nothing to do with his trouble breathing.

If Meg had a two-year-old, she'd gotten busy real quick after their separation. Unless…

A sharp pain stabbed his temple, and he braced his hands against the car, his head hanging between his arms. Unless she'd been busy *before* their separation.

No way. Meg was not the cheatin' kind. The other alternative stared him in the face. Planted itself in front of him like the Abominable Snowman howling for recognition.

Ian gulped at the cold, wet air, but couldn't fill his lungs. He grasped the car door handle, slippery with raindrops, and yanked. He fell on to the seat and dropped his forehead to the steering wheel.

The anger he'd felt at the thought of Meg having a child with another man couldn't even compare to the fear that now engulfed him. He had a son. And his name was Travis.

Chapter Five

"Ian?" Meg jerked her head to stare at her rock of a husband hunched over the steering wheel. He'd taken the news of Travis so calmly at the office. It must be hitting him now...like a sledgehammer from the looks of it. At least he'd held it together in front of Pete and the other deputies. Of course he'd hold it together in front of others. In that respect, they had the same steely resolve.

Her hand hovered over his curved back. Would he welcome her touch? Shrug it off? Go ballistic?

He rolled his head to the side, still planted against the steering wheel. "Travis is our son?"

"Y-yes. He's almost two and a half."

He groaned and closed his eyes. He'd barely reacted in the office when he found out. He had an amazing talent for suppressing his emotions, an amazing talent for compartmentalizing the different facets of his life. But now it looked as if those compartments were crashing together.

"You've had about an hour to get used to the idea. I'm kind of surprised you didn't yank me out of that office as soon as you found out." She thrust out her chin. "But then, you're good at shoving things to the corner and focusing on the here and now, especially when that here and now involves work."

Ian jerked upright and pounded the steering wheel with his fists. "I just figured it out, Meg. Just now. Just this minute."

"What?" Meg's jaw dropped. Now it was her turn for an emotional turmoil to whip through her body. "You just realized my son was *our* son? Who the hell did you imagine I'd been sleeping with when I was still with you?"

Ian's jaw worked, and then he passed an unsteady hand over his face. "I didn't think you'd been sleeping with anyone while we were together. I thought...I thought, I figured it was someone after our breakup."

She snorted. "I thought you were good at math. We've been apart just under three years."

He rubbed his eyes as if awakening from a crazy dream. "I don't know, Meg. I was thinking you had a baby, not a toddler."

"A baby on a tricycle? You really are clueless about kids." Her words extinguished the light in Ian's eyes, and his face blanched. She bit her lip and drew blood. She'd gone on the attack before he could lambast her for keeping their son a secret from him. She'd gone after him in the cruelest way, and instant tears sprang to her eyes.

"I'm sorry, Ian." She whispered into the hands that covered her mouth.

He grinned, a lopsided twist of his lips that never reached his green eyes, still slits of pain. "Don't be. You're right. You had every reason to keep the birth of our son a secret."

One tear spilled over and rolled down her cheek to catch on her index finger, scorching it. "I had foolish, selfish reasons for doing so. But I didn't start out with that plan in mind. I tried to reach you a few times at the beginning, but you were deep undercover."

"Story of my life, huh? I haven't been deep undercover for almost three years. Did you change your mind about telling me later? Did you ever plan to tell me about my son…*our* son?"

"Yes." She stroked his forearm, tense with corded muscle. "I thought about it every day."

I thought about you every day.

"Travis needs his father. I just wasn't sure…"

"You weren't sure I'd be there for him." He held up his hands to stop the protest bubbling to her lips. "When did you find out about your pregnancy?"

"After you left. After I realized you didn't want kids."

"You should've told me, Meg. I had the right to know, even if you believed I'd turn my back on you."

She curled her fingers around his, still white-knuckled and clenching the steering wheel. "I never thought that, Ian. I knew you'd come through for me, for us. I just didn't want to force you into anything. I didn't want to be a burden or a dreaded responsibility."

Her words had a hollow sound, and she threaded her fingers through his to soften the blow. She'd just confirmed his worst fears—that she considered Ian Dempsey unfit father material. How could she ever convey that her reluctance to tell him about Travis bubbled from her own insecurities and fears? She had an overriding terror of being dependent on anyone. She'd seen firsthand the price you had to pay for that dependence.

She scooped in a deep breath and opened her mouth, but Ian cut her off. "Save it, Meg. You had your reasons, and I don't want to hear any more of them."

Ian's jaw tightened as he cranked the engine of the rental car. He'd already transformed his hurt into anger. He'd pile it on top of all the other anger that formed the hard core of his soul.

"Now, which way to the hospital, so you can see your son before he's discharged?"

She didn't miss his reference to *your* son, but what did she expect? She'd cut Ian out of Travis's life. She couldn't expect him to brush that off or forgive her…ever.

She gave him directions to the hospital in Colorado Springs and settled into her seat while he plugged in his Bluetooth and called Colonel Scripps. As Ian exchanged information with the colonel, her ears almost twitched. Although she could hear only one side of the conversation, Ian's responses sounded cantankerous. She'd always assumed he held Colonel Scripps in great esteem, but what did she really know about that side of Ian's life?

Of course, the irritated edge to Ian's voice could have everything to do with the fact that he'd just found out he had a son she'd kept from him. The loss of his partner, Kayla, could be sinking in, too. From where she was sitting, it sounded like Colonel Scripps had several choice words for Ian and his handling of the assignment.

She sighed and leaned her head against the cool glass of the window. She'd often dreamed of the moment when she'd tell Ian about their son. Driving to the emergency room with the death of Ian's partner hanging over them and a covert mission in disarray somehow never entered those dreams.

Ian ended the call, yanked the Bluetooth out of his ear and scowled at the road. His short, dark hair capped off chiseled features as hard as granite. His erect posture, even cramped in a small sedan, spoke of Ian's military background and precise nature. Everything had a place in his life, and she'd just stepped in and mucked it all up for him.

"It didn't sound like the call went well."

He raised his shoulders in a stiff shrug. "Colonel Scripps told me he'd handle the arrangements for Kayla's body. I wanted to do it myself, finish what I started, but he wants me back on the case."

Yeah, Ian would want to wrap up all the loose ends himself. Because of the chaos of his childhood, he had ordered everything in his life just so. He gravitated toward the structure and discipline of the military like a drowning man to a life preserver.

She figured that's why he never filed for divorce. He didn't want that black mark on his record—the mental record he kept of a life in constant peril of slipping back into the abyss of disorder, disappointment and disaster.

She'd panicked at being sucked into that orbit of preciseness, so much like her father's world. The world she'd worked hard to escape, the world that had killed her mother and her twin sister.

"Turn left at the light." She jerked her thumb and then held onto the edge of the seat as Ian careened around the corner. "The hospital's up ahead on the left. I think the emergency entrance is the second driveway."

He followed her instructions, his lips pressed into a thin line. He seemed to grow madder by the minute. She fully expected to see steam seeping from his ears and nostrils. But that's as far as it would go. Ian didn't allow himself to get really angry.

The car bounced as it rolled over the speed bumps, and Ian swung into a parking space. He cut the engine and gripped the steering wheel as if ready for takeoff. "Do you want me to wait here?"

"No. It's time you met your son."

He blew out a harsh breath and pushed out of the car. Meg scrambled from her seat before he could open her door. She didn't want him attending to her, not after what she'd done to him.

The automatic doors whisked open for them, and Meg rushed to the intake desk. "I'm here to pick up my son, Travis Dempsey. Is he ready to go?"

The clerk tapped some keys on a keyboard and adjusted her glasses. "He's all done. Just a couple of stitches. He must be in the playroom next door."

"Thank you." Meg tripped across the polished linoleum, her knees weak and shaking. She didn't know if her anxiety stemmed from collecting Travis at the emergency room or from the first meeting of father and son.

She shoved open the swinging blue door, her gaze settling on Travis's dark head bent over a couple of Hot Wheels on the floor. Felicia rose from her chair, dropping her magazine. "I'm so sorry to give you such a scare, Meg. He's okay, but we should have kept him off that tricycle. The rubber is stripped off the pedal, and the edge cut him."

"I don't blame you, Felicia." Meg held open her arms as Travis spun around on his bottom and scrambled to his feet. "I've let him ride that tricycle before myself. Time to throw it out."

Travis's little legs pumped across the room until he threw himself into her arms. "Whoa, big guy. You don't want to open those stitches."

Leaning back in her arms, Travis jabbed a stubby finger at the red line beneath his chin. "Cut."

"I know." Meg gently touched her lips to the corner of his stitches. "You need to stop being such a daredevil, or you're going to get a lot more of these little stitches."

Meg rose to her feet, scooping up Travis in her arms. She nodded to Ian slouched against the wall, his eyes an unreadable dark green. "Felicia, this is Ian Dempsey, Travis's father. Felicia helps out at her mother's day care."

Only two bright spots of color on Felicia's cheeks betrayed her surprise. She smiled and held out her hand. "It's nice to meet you, Mr. Dempsey. Travis is a great kid."

With a visible effort Ian seemed to bite back the first comment that rose to his lips. "Good to meet you, too. I'm looking forward to discovering that for myself."

Travis's green eyes widened above the knuckle shoved firmly into his mouth. Had he understood already that this man was the father he'd just started to ask about?

Meg adjusted Travis on her hip and turned to Ian. "This is your son, Ian."

"I'm going to head home now, Meg. I'll leave the car seat we used for Travis in the waiting room. You can return it to the daycare when you get the chance. Nice meeting you, Mr. Dempsey." Felicia discreetly sidled out of the door, letting in a boy and a girl with their mother.

Ian took a tentative step forward and wedged a large finger beneath Travis's cut. "That's quite a battle scar there."

Travis's eyes got even bigger as he took in the larger-than-life man before him. Then he smiled around the finger still buried in his mouth.

"This is your daddy, Travis." Meg bounced him up and down a few times, but apparently Ian's presence still overwhelmed him. She shrugged. "Like most boys his age, he's not much of a talker yet. The girls his age are talking rings around him."

Ian smirked. "That won't change much, Travis."

"D-do you like his name?"

"Travis McGee, John D. MacDonald's character?"

Grinning, Meg nodded, feeling as if she'd at last done something right. Ian had loved the old pulp fiction of John D. MacDonald and his freewheeling P.I., Travis McGee. The name had been at the top of Meg's list.

"I like it." Ian clasped his hands awkwardly in front of him as if he didn't know what to do with them. Then he folded his arms across his chest, tucking his hands beneath his arms.

Did he think she was going to thrust Travis into his arms for some instant father-son bonding? Even for a child Travis's age, these things took time.

"Umm, I guess we'd better get going. I'm sure you have work to do, and I have a hike to lead tomorrow."

Ian pushed open the door and held it for her and Travis. "I don't think it's a great idea for you to be going on any more hikes for a while, Meg."

"Pfft. It's my job." She snapped her fingers. "I doubt if I'll have any more terrorists posing as tourists on my hike."

"How do you know?"

Meg crouched to retrieve the car seat Felicia had left by the front desk and almost toppled over at his words, a chill snaking along her spine. Ian snagged the car seat from her grasp.

"I'm sure if Hans Whatshisname returned to my hike I'd recognize him."

"We don't know if Hans is involved." He hoisted the car seat and trudged through the automatic doors. "We don't know if he's working with partners."

Meg straightened her shoulders, and Travis adjusted

his head. "I think it's best that I carry on as if I don't know anything...which I don't."

"You have a point." He ducked into the backseat of the car. "How do you hook this thing up?"

She grasped Travis beneath his armpits and peeled him off her body. "Here, take Travis a minute."

Meg's heart skipped several beats as she pressed her son against Ian's solid, unyielding chest. Would he refuse?

Ian opened his arms and wrapped them around Travis, his right arm supporting his bottom and his left securely pressed against his back. Travis was in no danger of falling out of Ian's protective embrace.

Meg bent forward and slid the seat belt through the anchors at the bottom of the car seat. She twisted her head over her shoulder. "Okay, hand him over. Time to get strapped in for takeoff, buddy."

Travis seemed as reluctant to leave his perch as Ian was to relinquish him. Before her heart leaped out of her chest, Meg cautioned herself. Easy, girl. Baby steps.

She settled Travis into his car seat, snapping the buckle between his legs. Then she kissed him on the chin. Yep, a daredevil—just like his father.

IAN GLANCED BETWEEN the road and the rearview mirror, adjusting it to get a better look at Travis...his son. *He looks like me.* The thought sent a shock wave through his body clear down to his hiking boots. Although, why should it surprise him? He'd contributed half his genes to the pool.

Occasionally, a pair of familiar green eyes met his in the mirror and Ian gave an encouraging smile. The boy had felt comfortable in his arms, like he belonged, just like holding his mother had always felt right.

After he'd gotten over the initial shock of discovering he had a two-year-old son, and after he'd finished excoriating himself for not being there for Travis, a seething rage bubbled to the surface. He'd kept a lid on his anger because he had no clue where it would lead, once uncapped.

His own father's anger had turned into abuse quickly enough, and Ian had always feared one followed on the heels of the other. Genes didn't lie.

At first, the thought that he'd missed his son's birth and the first two years of life shamed him so much he'd been willing to accept any excuse Meg laid at his door. Willing to cop to any attribute she threw at him. Then the anger settled into every fiber of his being. It didn't help that he knew her reasons had as much to do with her own messed up childhood as his own.

How could the two of them raise a child? His gaze stole to the mirror again and the brown-haired boy rewarded him with a toothy grin. Seemed like Meg had been doing just fine.

They cruised back into the small town of Crestville. "Did you leave your car at the foot of the trail?"

"Yes." She fiddled with the zipper of her jacket. "Do you want to join me and Travis for dinner tonight? Or… or are you too busy with the case?"

She'd turned his world upside down this afternoon and now she expected him to calmly have dinner with the son he'd just discovered? "Sure, I'll join you. Colonel Scripps sent an agent down from Denver to take care of Kayla, so I'll be meeting him later at the hospital we just left."

"Kayla was there?" She covered her mouth with a trembling hand.

"That's where they took her body."

"Did she have children, a husband?"

He closed his eyes briefly. "I don't know, Meg. She didn't reveal anything about herself other than her loyalty to Jack Coburn."

"Were they lovers?"

"I doubt it. Jack didn't mix business with pleasure, unlike Buzz. And look where it got him." Buzz had gotten involved with one of the translators who worked with Prospero. A beauty named Raven, whose name matched her glossy black hair. But they hadn't lasted long.

"Did Buzz and that woman split up?"

"Occupational hazard." He parked the car and jerked his thumb over his shoulder. "He's out."

She smiled and her entire face softened and glowed with an ethereal light—*motherhood.* "He must be exhausted after all the excitement. I'll make sure he has a nice nap before dinner, so you can spend some time getting to know him. I have a lot of lost time to make up to you."

"We all do."

Meg indicated her car and Ian crouched into the backseat of his rental and scooped up Travis's car seat with Travis still strapped inside and carried him to Meg's car. He slid it onto the backseat of her SUV, next to the other car seat, without Travis even blinking an eye.

Meg straightened up after securing Travis, a rosy color blooming in her cheeks. She looked exactly as he remembered her on Everest the first time he saw her… minus the red nose and chattering teeth. She reached into her pocket and pulled out a scrap of paper. "Here's my address. Will you be finished around seven?"

"Seven will work. Do you want me to bring anything?

Wine? Dessert? Milk?" He pointed to the sleeping Travis, his dark lashes like tiny crescents on his cheeks.

Meg laughed. "I have everything covered. See you then."

Meg drove off and Ian released the pent-up air in his lungs. Land mines dotted this unchartered territory—one false step and he'd turn into his father.

Ian returned to his car and slid open his cell phone. He needed to hook up with the agent from Denver and then play Hide the Covert Op from the Covert Operative. Colonel Scripps and all of the Prospero team members had agreed to keep their mission under wraps. One hitch in their plans could send the wrong signal to Jack's captors. Until they knew more about Jack's situation, they planned to be tight-lipped about this one.

After a few hours of playing footsie with the spook and exchanging glares with Sheriff Cahill, Ian returned to his hotel with a headache pounding behind his eyes. He shrugged out of his down vest, his hand skimming a hard object tucked in the inside pocket.

He withdrew Kayla's camera with his heart thudding, making his head throb even more. He flicked the button on the back to the picture viewer position and the camera whirred to life—must've dried off. With his mouth dry, Ian clicked through the pictures, studying each frame on the small screen.

Kayla had managed to take a picture of every hiker on that trip. The German looked like any other tourist, eagerly taking photos of the impressive scenery and posing, smiling and unaffected, for Kayla.

Ian peered at the pictures of the waterfall and his breath came out in short spurts. She'd taken these moments before she went over. Had she seen something? He sucked in a breath. The last photo showed Kayla, laughing, holding her hands in front of her. The killer must've taken this shot. Why? To get next to her to push her over?

He pressed the button to close the camera and tossed it onto the credenza. He'd get prints of those pictures and blow them up. Something about that spot or Kayla's activities had set this guy off.

Checking his watch, he slipped it from his wrist. He had another ordeal in front of him. Pausing in front of the mirror he moved in for a closer inspection. Dark lashes framed green eyes, brown hair cropped close to tame the unruly waves. Another face appeared superimposed upon his, one dark curl hanging above a pair of sleepy eyes.

No. His son would never be an ordeal. He'd manage. He'd figure it out somehow, even if he had to watch a million sappy TV shows to find the proper role model for fatherhood.

He'd spent a lifetime distancing himself from his father. He didn't plan to travel the same road with his own son.

Ian hit the shower and positioned his shoulder blades under the spray of hot water. Kids had to be similar to animals—instinctive, feral, unpolished by society's constraints. Show a kid a face of fear, and he'd sense it and go in for the kill.

Once out of the shower, Ian pulled on a pair of jeans, a long-sleeve T-shirt and a flannel shirt. He stuffed his feet into a lighter pair of hiking boots and grabbed his wallet. He still had time to stop by the little shop next to the hotel to find something for Travis.

He was not above bribery.

He picked out a toy train that clacked when you pulled it as the wheels went around. The store clerk wrapped it in tissue paper and Ian set off for Meg's house and the most important dinner of his life.

He drove through the downtown of Crestville and switched on his brights when he hit the country road leading away from the town. He could picture Meg out here, but the nights must get lonely.

Not that he'd mind easing her loneliness. Did she still feel their attraction as strongly as he did? Every touch of her hand today, every whiff of her sweet scent caused indecent thoughts to charge through his brain and his libido.

Her bombshell today about Travis had tempered most of those thoughts...for about an hour. Who was he kidding? He'd bed the woman ten minutes after she stole all his money and left him for dead. She was in his blood.

He slowed at each mailbox, picking out the addresses with his headlights until he saw her house number reflecting in the dark. He pulled into the gravel driveway and parked behind her silver SUV. Her porch light created a golden arc in front of her house, where more light glowed from the windows. She'd created a homey setting for Travis—unlike her own upbringing in cold, palatial mansions and boarding schools.

He cut the engine and leaned across the seat to retrieve his gift for Travis. Then he slid from the car and froze.

The quiet of the night stole over him, but the hairs on the back of his neck stood at attention. He strained his ears to hear the sound again, his nostrils flaring.

Then he heard it. Twigs snapped and crispy fall leaves crunched beneath stealthy footsteps. He zeroed in on the dark underbrush past the lights and warmth of Meg's house. A bush rustled.

It could be an animal. Ian took two steps toward the

porch and the noises grew closer together as if something...or someone had just picked up the pace of its retreat.

The foliage crackled and snapped, acting like a prod on Ian. He launched forward, blindly running toward the back of the house. He halted at the edge of the underbrush, his eyes growing accustomed to the darkness.

For such a short sprint, his breath burned his lungs. He cocked his head, only his ragged breathing and a few displaced crickets answered him. He must have terrified that animal. He shook his head and turned toward the house. Then something caught his eye.

He leaned forward to pinch between his two fingers a piece of crimped, black yarn dangling from a twig. He wrapped the yarn around his finger and held it close to his face.

If that was an animal, it had just lost a handmade scarf.

Chapter Six

Meg tweaked the final lily in the vase and inhaled its languid scent. She'd prepared for this dinner as if it were a first date instead of an appointment to introduce a father to his long-lost son.

Would the flowers scare off Ian? Would the candlelight? Would the look of unabashed desire in her eyes?

Dusting her hands together, she turned to Travis who was idly turning the pages of a picture book, still sleepy from his nap. She had to focus on the real purpose of this dinner. She leaned forward and blew out the two candles flickering on the table.

A movement at the kitchen window caught her eye. The yellow curtain floated over the sink, and she scuffed to the kitchen in slippers to close the window. She slid the window across its track and jumped when it snapped shut.

Her own wide eyes stared back at her and she puffed out a breath, fogging the glass. She thought she'd seen a face at the window, but it must've been her own. There would be no reason for Ian to come to the back of the house when she'd put the porch light on to illuminate the front door.

She opened the fridge and grabbed a chilled bottle of wine. She could use a glass before Ian showed up on her doorstep. A rap at the door, and the sweating bottle almost slipped from her hand. This visit had her on edge.

Glancing at her fuzzy slippers, she gasped. Maybe she didn't want to go overboard with candles, but she didn't want to dress down too much for the occasion.

Travis peeked over the top of his book. "Door, Mommy."

"I know, sweets. Give me a minute." Meg scurried into her bedroom, kicked off the slippers and stuffed her feet into a pair of clogs.

By the time she returned to the living room, Ian was banging on the front door, calling her name. Travis had rolled off the couch and run to the door, hanging on to the doorknob.

What had gotten into Ian? Meg hitched Travis under one arm and peered through her peephole to verify the maniac huffing and puffing at her door was really her husband. She then clicked the dead bolt and opened the door.

Ian's gaze swept the length of her body as if to make sure she was really standing in front of him and then ran a hand through his short hair. "What took you so long?"

"Uh, I was in the middle of something. What's the matter with you?" She swung the door open and ushered him inside, placing Travis on the carpet.

"Nothing. Just seemed like you took a long time." He shoved a hand in his pocket and withdrew it quickly.

He must be as nervous as she was about this encounter. Did he have a trickle of sweat on his forehead? It had to be below forty degrees outside.

"How are you doing?" Ian dropped to his knees and

touched a gentle fingertip to Travis's chin. "How's that battle scar?"

Travis grinned and poked at his own cheek. "Babble scar."

Ian laughed and the sound did funny things to Meg's insides. For all of Ian's fear of children, he seemed to have a handle on this.

"Babble scars? I think your mom has a few of those." Ian opened and closed his hand in a yacking sign.

"Hey." She kneed him in the back. "Don't spoil Travis's illusion. He thinks I'm perfect."

Ian stretched to his full height and raised one eyebrow. "I used to think that, too."

Meg felt the smile dissolve from her face. Ian would never forgive her. "I'm trying, Ian, right here and right now."

He rubbed a hand across a freshly-shaved chin. "I appreciate that Meg, but you sucker-punched me. And you told me right here and right now because you didn't have a choice. I stumbled back into your life and I overheard a telephone conversation."

He had her there. She should've tried harder to reconnect, but her old demons had grabbed hold of her and whispered their warnings in her ear. She sucked in her trembling lip.

"Are you hungry?"

"Starving. Does Travis eat with us?"

She waved a hand at Travis's high chair pulled up to the table. "He's going to graduate to a booster seat soon. He's tall for his age."

"Do you have some baby pictures to share?"

"I have tons, and I can give you a bunch." She let the sentence hang in the air. Would she be giving him a bunch of Travis's baby pictures when he left them?

"Oh, I almost forgot." He held out the package he'd been clutching to his side since he walked into the house. "Something for Travis."

Travis eyed the package and held out his hands. "Gimme."

Meg rolled her eyes. "You'll have to excuse Travis. We haven't gotten to social graces yet. We're still working on not throwing food at the dinner table."

"One thing at a time." Ian placed the gift in Travis's outstretched hands while Meg reminded him to say "thank you," which he did after a fashion.

Travis ripped through the filmy tissue paper and squealed when he held the little wooden train in his hands. He twirled the wheel with his finger and laughed at the clacking noise.

"That's cute. Travis, you have to eat dinner before playing with your new train." She took the toy from his hands. "I'll put it next to you at the table."

As she lifted Travis into his high chair, Ian sauntered into the kitchen after hanging up his jacket. "Need anything?"

"You can open that wine on the counter and pour a couple of glasses." Once she secured Travis in his chair, she squeezed past Ian in the small kitchen and opened the refrigerator door. She slid the salad bowl from a shelf and plucked two bottles of salad dressing from the door. After placing them on the table, she scooped some chili from the pot on the stove into a ceramic bowl and carried it to the table.

"Do you have some matches?" Ian pointed to the two candlesticks on the table. "Unless that's too dangerous for Travis."

Meg suppressed a smile. "Matches in the first drawer on the right when you walk into the kitchen. Travis can't reach these candles, especially strapped into his chair. Can you please grab that basket of cornbread, too?"

After Ian had plopped the basket in the center of the table and lit the candles, he studied the wine label. "White wine with chili? What would your father say?"

Meg snorted. "Who gives a...?" She slid a glance toward Travis, busy mashing cornbread on his tray.

"Sorry for bringing up a sore subject." He tipped more wine into her glass, even though she'd just taken one sip, probably to compensate for mentioning her father and spoiling a perfectly good meal.

She took a gulp and began spooning beans and little pieces of meat onto Travis's tray, along with some thoroughly cooked carrots.

"That's not too spicy for you?" Ian tapped Travis's high chair with his fork.

Meg liked the way Ian spoke directly to Travis instead of over his head. Travis liked it, too. He wasn't much of a conversationalist, but he studied Ian with interest.

Travis repeated, "Spicy," and then crammed more beans into his mouth.

"There's your answer." Meg laughed and felt the tension seeping from her shoulders for the first time that evening.

They shared another few glasses of wine and Ian and Travis got into a very serious discussion about colors, until it all dissolved into silliness, with Ian accusing Travis of having a blue face.

Travis had always had men in his life, mostly Meg's coworkers, and lately Pete Cahill, but he seemed to sense something special in Ian. Could it be that blood connection? Probably not, since Ian had felt no such connection with his own father.

It was all Ian.

When Travis started to get antsy, Meg wiped his red-stained face and hands and scooped him from the high chair. She handed him his train and deposited him on the floor with a sippy cup of milk.

The clink of dishes in the sink indicated that Ian had already cleared the table. He'd been a stellar husband in that respect, since he couldn't stand clutter. She gathered the remaining food from the table and joined him in the kitchen.

He bumped his hip against hers. "Just like old times, huh?"

"You were always a big help around the house...when you were home."

"Ouch." He slid the last plate into the dishwasher and wiped his hands on a dishtowel, crumpling it in his fists. "That's why you didn't tell me you were pregnant?"

Sighing, she flipped her hair over her shoulder. "I had a million reasons, Ian. All of them seemed rock solid at the time. Now that I see you and Travis together...I realize I made a mistake. A big one."

Such a big one, she'd probably torpedoed any chance of getting back together with her husband. She folded her arms across her stomach, wondering how that idea had wormed itself into her brain. She'd never dreamed of reuniting with Ian, even after telling him about Travis. Probably because she knew, once she dropped that bombshell, he'd never be able to forgive her.

"Okay, no more." He held up his fingers in a peace sign. "No more third degree. I'm going to take what I can get now, and spend some time with my son."

He dropped the dishtowel on the counter and joined Travis on the floor. Meg left them together while she finished cleaning up the kitchen. She checked the latch on the window above the sink. Usually she enjoyed a little fresh air, even cold fresh air, but the night seemed particularly black outside, with the clouds skittering over a tiny slice of moon.

She shivered for no good reason and then punched the buttons on the dishwasher. Her son's whining indicated bedtime.

Crouching next to Travis on the floor, she ruffled his toffee-colored hair. Would it turn into a darker brown like Ian's? "I think someone's getting tired."

Ian fell back on his forearms. "Oh good. I thought it was me."

"Kids get fussy when they get tired, at least this kid does." She pinched Travis's nose. "Time for bed. Can you say good-night to…Daddy?"

Travis clambered onto Ian's stomach, knocking him flat on his back. Then he bounced on his ribs as Ian grunted. "What am I, a horse?"

Giggling, Travis fell forward and burrowed his small head into Ian's very broad chest. Ian brushed a tentative hand across Travis's scalp, twisting one curl around his finger. "Ah, he has the curse of the wavy hair."

"Curse? Everyone loves his hair." Meg tickled Travis's cheek. "You ready for bed now?"

Travis nodded and Meg peeled him from Ian's body. As she balanced him on her hip, Travis waved. "Night, Daddy."

Meg's throat ached and she blinked back tears.

Ian waved back. "Night, Travis."

By the time Meg brushed Travis's teeth and changed him into his jammies, he was half asleep. She tucked him into his brand-new toddler bed. *Toddler beds and booster seats already,* and Ian had missed it all.

Damn her insecurities.

She kicked off her clogs and padded into the living

room in her stocking feet. Ian had a glass of water in one hand while twisting something around the fingers of his other hand.

She poured herself a glass of water and joined him on the other end of the couch. "You're doing great with Travis, very natural."

His lips quirked up on one side. "It helps that I don't actually have to carry on a conversation with him."

"Oh, I don't know." She tucked her feet beneath her. "That discussion of the different colors sounded quite profound to me." She tilted her head toward the yarn wrapped around his fingers. "What's that?"

He unraveled the black yarn and dangled it from his fingertips. "I found it outside."

"Huh?" She wrinkled her nose. "And you picked it up?"

He pulled the yarn taut and strummed it with his thumb. "When I walked up to your house tonight, I heard something in the bushes."

Meg's pulse hitched and her heart fluttered in her chest as her gaze darted to the kitchen window. "The underbrush at the back of the house?"

"Yeah. I thought it might be an animal, even though I had a weird feeling about it. The noise sounded too calculated to be random."

"Calculated how?"

"A rustling. Silence. Twigs cracking. Silence. And then an all-out burst of activity when I started walking back there. If my car had frightened an animal, it would've hightailed it out of there immediately."

Meg folded her arms, her fingers biting into her biceps. "You walked back there?"

He nodded.

Her heart was beating so hard, the blood thrummed in her ears. "And you found that?"

Ian dropped the yarn on her leg, where it seemed to burn through her jeans. "Is it yours? Do you recognize it?"

She pinched it between two fingers, the texture rough on her pads. "It looks like a piece of yarn unraveled from a scarf or some mittens, doesn't it?"

"That's what I thought."

"You think someone was out there?"

He shrugged, carefully avoiding her eyes. "Could've been there before. Is that a path people normally take?"

Swallowing hard, she shook her head. "That way pretty much leads to wilderness, or the house next door. But if you're going to the houses along this stretch, you use the road out front. You don't scramble through the bushes in the back."

Ian held out his hand and Meg dropped the yarn, now scorching her fingers, into his palm. "That's why you pounded on my door, isn't it?"

"It's dark and deserted out here, Meg."

She folded her hands in her lap to stop their trembling. "I think I saw a face at the kitchen window right before you arrived."

"What?" He jerked forward, banging his knee on the coffee table and sloshing the water over the rim of the glass.

"I was setting the table and the curtains stirred. When I went over to shut the window, I thought I saw a face."

"Why didn't you say something?"

"I figured I imagined it. Why didn't you say something about the noises in the underbrush and the yarn before now?"

He hunched forward, balancing his elbows on his knees. "The threat, if that's what it was, had disappeared for the moment. I didn't want to ruin dinner. I didn't want to scare you or Travis. Besides," he pointed to the closet by the door, "I have my weapon in my jacket."

"They haven't found the German tourist yet." Meg drew her knees to her chest and wrapped her arms around her legs, hugging them tightly.

"What about his hotel room? His car?"

"I don't know about the hotel room. His car is still in the lot at the trailhead. Has the CIA checked out his identity yet?"

"The agent down from Denver ran a check on all the hikers on the list from Rocky Mountain Adventures. No hits. But Hans could have appropriated someone's identity."

"Great." Closing her eyes, she tilted her head back.

Strong fingers squeezed her knee. "Meg? I don't want to leave you and Travis here alone tonight."

Her eyelids flew open. She'd been longing to hear those words all night, but not under the present circumstances. Not under any circumstances where Ian would feel obligated to stay with her. He'd always fulfill his duty, but she didn't want him that way.

"I think we're good, Ian. We're not even sure there was ever anyone lurking around outside. All we have is a piece of yarn and a phantom face at the window that could've been my own."

His hand slid from her leg. "I don't like it."

"Besides, I have a gun, too, and I know how to use it. I keep it unloaded and locked up for Travis's safety, but I can pull it out."

Ian's eyes narrowed to cold slits and Meg pressed her spine against the cushion of the couch. "Why are you pushing me away, Meg? I can bunk right here. I'm not interested in sharing your bed. It's not just about you anymore. I have a son in there, and I'm here to protect him."

His words lashed her face and she dropped her head, allowing her hair to create a veil around her hot cheeks. She had her answer right there. He wanted his son but not her. "You can stay."

A noisy sigh escaped his lips and one long finger hooked around the edge of her hair, sweeping it back from her face and tracing the curve of her ear. "I'm sorry, Meg. I'm on edge."

Ian had never been quick to anger, and once it boiled over he worked quickly to suck it back in. He'd seen too much anger and violence in his life to let it get the better of him. Meg knew the discovery that he had a son had tested his reserve.

She jerked away from his gentle touch and pushed up from the couch. "I'll get you a blanket and pillow. I'm afraid you are going to have to sleep here, since we have only two bedrooms."

"I've slept on worse."

She gathered an extra blanket from the hall cupboard and snagged one of her own pillows off her bed. Clutching them to her chest, she returned to the living room where Ian had unlaced his boots and was yanking them off his feet.

She dropped the bedding at the end of the couch. "Do you really think my visitor tonight has anything to do with what happened on the mountain today?"

"Not sure." He shook out the blanket and collected the water glasses from the coffee table. "If our boy, Hans, is still missing, he could be anywhere. And he obviously knows who you are. Maybe he thinks you saw something, too."

"I hope not." She wrapped her arms around her body. She'd hiked those mountain trails numerous times and never feared beast or nature. It took a man to make her blood run cold in her veins.

Ian stepped over the coffee table with one long stride and enveloped her in a warm embrace. His gesture shocked her into silence and immobility. When he stroked the back of her hair, she melted against him... just a little.

"I should never have used your tour group. God knows, I never meant to drag you into my operation."

"Maybe it was fate." She rested her cheek against his chest where his heart beat strong and steady. "You discovered your son."

His lips brushed her hair before he pulled away and whispered, "Fate."

Before she made a fool of herself and begged him to kiss her, or worse, to take her to bed, she laid her palms flat on his chest and stumbled backward. He caught her arm, but she couldn't even tolerate that level of contact with him if he didn't intend on taking it any further.

"I need to get to bed. I still have that hike tomorrow morning."

Ian opened his mouth, thought better of it, and lifted his shoulders. "I'll be right here."

Meg turned away on a pair of unsteady legs.

"Thanks for dinner and thanks for allowing me time with Travis."

She halted but didn't turn around. Then she called over her shoulder as her feet dragged toward the hallway. "Don't ever thank me for that."

MEG CHANGED INTO her pajamas and crept into the bathroom to wash her face and brush her teeth. When she poked her head out of the door, she heard Ian's heavy breathing. He could fall asleep faster than any human she knew.

Since she had every intention of leading that hike tomorrow, she shoved her feet into her slippers and tiptoed into the kitchen to the door that led to the attached garage. She wanted to check her pack so she'd be ready to go in the morning.

She slipped the lock from the top of the door and descended the two steps into the garage, flicking on the light when she reached the bottom. Cold air wrapped chilly fingers around her body and she shivered in her lightweight flannel pajamas. She scooted past Travis's new tricycle, the one he should've been riding at day care today, and nudged a few balls out of the way with the toe of her slipper.

Something crunched beneath her feet. A gust of wind tousled her hair. Her brows drew together and she twisted her head to the side.

Then her jaw dropped and she let loose a scream to match the howling wind.

Chapter Seven

Ian jerked awake. Branches from the naked plum tree out front tapped against the window. He punched the pillow and shifted his body, draping his legs over the side of the couch. Hard to get comfortable trying to cram a six-foot-two frame onto a six-foot couch. Too bad he'd woken up.

Why did he wake up? Usually he slept like the dead, unless… He held his breath. The wind screeched outside—and something screeched inside.

He scrambled from his uncomfortable bed, grabbed his gun from beneath the couch and stumbled toward the back rooms. Travis's door gaped open, but the boy slumbered peacefully, his breathing soft and regular. Ian lurched across the hall toward Meg's room and then spun around at the commotion behind him.

Meg barreled down the dark hallway, arms thrust in front of her. "Ian? Ian?"

"It's me." He grabbed her hands, shoving his weapon in the waistband of his jeans. "I'm here."

She twisted one hand out of his grasp and pointed toward the living room. "The garage. Someone broke into the garage."

His gut twisted. He should've checked out the house

when he got here and suspected someone had been lurking outside. "He's not still there, is he?"

"God, I hope not." She peeked into Travis's room, checked the windows and left his door wide open. "I saw the broken window and then after a few moments of shock, flew out of that garage so fast I almost lost my fuzzy slippers."

"Did you scream?" He curled an arm around her shoulders and led her back to the living room. "I heard a scream."

"Yep, that was me."

A tremble rolled through her body and he tucked her against his side before planting her on his tumbled bed. He slid his gun up his bare chest and then dangled it at his side. "Which way's the garage?"

Her gaze jumped from the gun to his face and back again. She leveled a surprisingly steady finger toward the kitchen. "It's through that door. The broken window is on the right side of the garage as you enter."

She gasped and he nearly fired into the microwave. "Watch your bare feet. There's glass all over the floor."

Blowing out a breath he perched on the edge of the coffee table and pulled on his heavy socks. "These will have to do."

His steps whispered across the tiled floor of the kitchen and he slid the lock back on the door. Meg hovered at the entrance to the kitchen. "Hit the light switch on your right."

He flicked on the light and scanned the garage. Meg didn't park her car in here, but all sorts of mountain climbing equipment, outdoor tools and toys crammed the small space. She even had a kayak hanging from the rafters.

Not many places for a man to hide. Ian bounded down

the two steps and picked his way across the floor littered with toys and balls and then glass. He squatted next to the pieces of broken window.

The guy had hit the window hard. A glass-cutting device would've been neater, but then he probably didn't imagine that this assignment would involve breaking and entering.

Ian peered at the jagged edges around the window. No way anyone climbed through those spiky teeth. Whoever broke that window didn't have time to remove the pieces of glass and crawl through.

Had Ian interrupted him when he arrived at Meg's place?

His gut roiled when he thought about what might have happened if he hadn't come to dinner tonight. And stayed? Was the man watching the house now? Had he planned to come back and finish what he started?

Like hell he would.

"Ian?" Meg's voice floated down to him and the edge of fear in it pumped a fresh load of adrenaline into his system.

"It's all good. Nobody hiding out down here. He probably couldn't find any room."

Ian climbed the two steps, shut off the light and locked the door behind him. At least she had a good, solid one-way dead bolt.

Meg stood, one ridiculous fuzzy slipper on top of the other, hovering between the kitchen and the living room. "Do you think he was in there? I didn't want to stick around to see if he took anything."

Ian put the safety back on his gun and placed it on the kitchen counter. "He didn't get through that window. He didn't remove the shards of glass still in the frame. Nobody would've been able to crawl through that."

"Oh." Meg's tensed shoulders dropped. "Do you think he wanted to get in?"

He wanted to take her in his arms again. She looked vulnerable in her soft, flowered pajamas and bunny slippers. Vulnerable? *She kept your son from you.*

Ian rubbed his eyes. "I don't know, Meg. Do you have much vandalism in this area? Kids pulling pranks?"

"That's what you think now?" Her eyes widened. "Kids pulling pranks? Don't try to spare me, Ian. If you think some terrorist has me in his sights because he thinks I know something or have something, spit it out."

Wedging his palms on the countertop, he hunched forward. "Just seems like a coincidence to me. Kayla dies, we stay behind to hike out and you have a Peeping Tom breaking windows in your house. What does it sound like to you?"

"Sounds like I've stepped in it." She shook her foot in front of her. "Fuzzy slippers and all."

He laughed and slapped the counter. That's what he loved...*liked* about Meg. She could be terrified, facing a crevasse that tumbled away into nothingness, and she'd scrounge up a little bit of humor for the situation.

"In the morning, I'll take a look around outside and see if our visitor left anything besides the yarn from his scarf. Somehow, I can't picture him wearing mittens." On the way to his makeshift bed, he chucked Meg under the chin. "Get some sleep."

"Are you comfortable enough on the couch?"

"I was fine until you screamed." He peeled off his socks and adjusted the blanket over his shoulders. "Good night, Meg."

"Good night." She shuffled from the room and he could tell by the squeak of a hinge, she was checking on Travis again.

She had the mom stuff all figured out. But right now, it wasn't the mom stuff that made his mouth water every time she smiled or touched his hand. Ian punched his pillow a few times and turned his face into the soft cotton of the pillowcase, inhaling the sweet wildflower scent of his wife.

THE FOLLOWING MORNING a bug crawling across Ian's face woke him up. He slapped at it and burrowed deeper into the pillow, trying to recapture his erotic dream about Meg, featuring a field of wildflowers and a lot of bare skin.

The bug resumed its course across his cheek, and Ian smacked it again eliciting…giggles.

Dishes clinked in the sink. "Travis, leave your daddy alone. He's sleeping."

Ian peeled open one eye and met an identical green one staring back at him. He yawned and Travis poked a little finger into his gaping mouth. Ian snapped his mouth around the finger, holding it tight with his lips.

Travis squealed but made no attempt to remove his finger, instead wiggling it behind Ian's teeth. Ian spit out the finger, making a face by screwing up his eyes and puckering his lips. "Ugh, I almost swallowed a bug."

The "bug" giggled again as Ian hunched up to a sitting position. He grabbed Travis beneath the arms and hauled him onto the couch next to him.

Meg wedged a shoulder against the entrance to the kitchen, cradling a cup of steaming coffee. "Is he bothering you?"

"Not at all." Ian trailed his fingers through his son's curls, his gaze tracking up and down Meg's outfit of jeans and hiking boots. She obviously had no intention of following his advice. "Apparently, it's time to get up anyway."

"I made coffee, hot and strong, just the way you like it. There are some blueberry waffles on the stove and juice and fruit in the fridge." She waved an arm behind her. "Help yourself. I'm dropping Travis off at Eloise's Day Care—Eloise is Felicia's mother. Then I'm going to work."

At this last statement, she squared her shoulders and planted her boots about two feet apart. He knew better than to go on the attack. Besides, he had his own methods. Hadn't he been a covert ops guy under the best damn leader in the entire military?

"Mmm, I love blueberry waffles."

Meg almost spit her coffee back into her cup. "I made them last weekend. They're frozen. Just pop them in the microwave for a minute."

Travis scrambled from his lap and trotted toward a small backpack with a superhero on it. Ian would have to brush up on his superheroes.

"I can handle a microwave." He stretched and the blanket fell away from his body. Meg's eyes flicked over his chest and her gaze felt like the brush of a soft feather. A hot need plunged from his belly further south. He and Meg had always liked to start the day making love.

Ian cleared his throat and yanked the blanket across his crotch. "What trail are you hiking today?"

"Morningside." If she'd noticed his lust springing into action, she gave no sign other than spinning around toward the kitchen and dropping her cup in the sink. "What are you doing today?"

"First I'm going to check outside that garage window and the surrounding area. Maybe our boy left a calling card." He pushed off the couch, shook out the blanket and folded it. "Then I'm going to do some more checking up on those hikers from yesterday."

Meg grabbed her pack by the straps and hoisted it over her shoulders. "Thanks for sticking around last night, Ian. If you had left and I discovered that window…well, I probably would've stayed up all night pacing. I felt safe with you here."

"I'm glad I could make you feel safe." He took two steps toward her and hooked his thumbs around the backpack straps skimming the sides of her breasts. "Now stay that way."

A pink tide inched across her cheeks. "Get your backpack, Travis."

Travis scooped up his pack and hitched it over his shoulders just like Mom. Then he scurried to the two of them and grabbed Ian around the leg.

Ian swept him up in his arms, superhero backpack and all. "You have a great day, kiddo. No more battle scars, at least for now."

He followed Meg to the front door, still clasping Travis to his chest, Travis's hair tickling his chin. The fact that he'd been half-responsible for creating this miracle filled him with awe. How could anyone abuse that gift? How had his parents managed to live with themselves?

"I'll take him from here." Meg held out her arms.

"Are you sure?" Ian didn't feel like relinquishing his hold on his son. He had a sudden, irrational fear that if he let him go now, he'd have to wait another two years before seeing him again.

"You're hardly dressed to go out into a brisk Colorado morning." She waved her fingers at his bare chest and feet.

"You have a point." He gave Travis one last squeeze

before turning him over to Meg. "Be careful, Meg. Beware of German tourists bearing gifts."

"Back atcha."

Ian folded his arms across his chest as the cold air needled his flesh, giving rise to a rash of goose bumps. He watched Meg secure Travis in his car seat and back out of the driveway. When the last puff of exhaust disappeared, he turned and shut the door.

He'd throw on his clothes here, and then shower at the hotel. Just as soon as he devoured a couple of those blueberry waffles. He poured himself a cup of black coffee and sipped it as he tossed a waffle into the microwave. After making short work of not one, but two waffles smothered in maple syrup, he finished dressing and braced against the chilly air to investigate the back of Meg's house.

She lived on the edge of the wilderness. Rough terrain rushed up to the back of her house and then became civilized as it met the patterned bricks of her patio. She needed a fence around her property to keep animals, human and otherwise, away from the house.

Ian stepped up to the broken window, searching the ground beneath it. A few sprinkles of glass sparkled on the bricks, but most had landed inside the garage. At six-feet-two, he couldn't even see into the garage, and would definitely have a hard time hoisting himself over the ledge.

He surveyed the patio, noting the wooden table, chairs and a folded umbrella. The intruder probably used one of the chairs to reach the window and then shoved it back under the table when his plans changed abruptly.

Ian stepped off the bricks to the dirt path along the side of the house, the same path he'd followed last night. He couldn't be sure which bush snagged the yarn from the scarf, so he studied the foliage for a broken line into the underbrush. A few broken twigs, a few misshapen leaves and a big wet footprint in the dirt—his—marked the spot.

Parting the branches, he ducked into the foliage. The hostile environment scratched and clawed at him from all sides, but he could discern a ramshackle and recent trail. He pushed his way through until he stumbled into a clearing.

Another house, similar to Meg's, the front leading to the same road, arose out of the apparent wilderness. No startled residents met him or attempted to stop him, so he traipsed through the backyard to the front of the house. Yep—Meg's nearest neighbor.

Ian peered up and down the road. The intruder could've parked his car along the side or ensconced it in one of the turnouts down the way. *Whatever.* Ian had missed his opportunity last night, and the guy hadn't left anymore tell-tale signs. Now if he could just remember if Hans, the German tourist, had been wearing a black knit scarf.

He trudged back up the road to Meg's house and slipped inside. He washed up the dishes she'd left in the sink and rinsed out the coffeepot. Then he gathered his stuff and hit the road.

Morningside Trail. He could find it. He could hike it. He could follow Meg. And he could do it a lot faster than she could, with a passel of dawdling tourists holding her back.

Ian pulled his rental into the parking lot of his hotel. The place would be packed during ski season, but Crestline was still on the cusp between fall and winter and hadn't had the first snowfall yet. Bad enough the climbers and hikers had descended en masse. He didn't need a crowd of skiers to complicate this mission any more.

Of course, the minute Meg showed up as the guide for the hike, the mission had gone downhill from there. The mission maybe, but not his life. He had a son. And despite everything, a smile stole over his entire face.

Jingling his keys in the pocket of his jacket, he waved to the clerk at the front desk and caught the elevator to the third floor. A housekeeping cart hunched at the end of the hallway, abandoned by its keeper. He and Kayla had adjoining rooms. He swallowed hard as he passed hers. He and the agent from Denver decided to keep Kayla's death under wraps, and Rocky Mountain Adventures hadn't objected. The tourists on Meg's hike might have spread the word in town, but nobody official would confirm it.

Ian dragged the key card out of his pocket and inserted it into the slot. At the green light, he pushed open the door and flipped up the light switch. His nostrils flared at the scent of tobacco. He'd specifically requested a non-smoking room. Both of his parents had been chain smokers, and the stench of tobacco made him nauseous.

His gaze tracked around the room, taking in an open drawer, a tossed pillow and a stack of hotel literature fanned across the credenza. A chill rippled across his flesh and he reached for his gun.

He crept forward, nudging the bathroom door with the toe of his boot. It stopped. With his heart thudding a dirge in his chest, he peered around the edge of the door.

He was sure he hadn't left that body on the floor.

Chapter Eight

Ian dropped to his knees and pressed two fingers against the hotel maid's pencil-thin neck. Her body was folded over the side of the tub, a sponge still wedged in her gloved hand. A trickle of blood meandered down the side of her face, taking a detour into her ear.

Her pulse ticked, faint but steady, beneath the pads of his fingers. He loosened her frame from the edge of the bathtub and stretched her out on the floor, her gangling legs extending into the entryway to the bathroom.

He stepped over her, grabbed the phone and dialed 911. Then he called the front desk and explained the situation to the clerk, who started hyperventilating. Good thing he'd called 911 first.

Crouching beside the maid again, he rolled up a bath towel and nudged it beneath her head. He cranked on the faucet in the tub and pulled a washcloth from the shelf above the toilet. The cool water soaked the cloth as Ian held it beneath the faucet. When he'd saturated it, he wrung it out and dabbed the maid's pale cheeks and lips. He now noticed the blood on her face was oozing from a lump on the side of her head.

Footsteps thumped down the hallway, stopping at Ian's hotel room. Then the thumping started on the door. Ian lodged the washcloth against the lump on the maid's head and swung open the door.

"What happened? Is Crystal okay?"

"I wouldn't say she's okay." Ian gestured toward Crystal's unconscious form laid out on the bathroom floor. "But she's alive."

The elevator doors trundled open, launching three EMTs into the hallway, whisking a stretcher and medical equipment along with them. Ian pushed the door open wider and waved. "She's in here."

While the EMTs crowded into the bathroom, Ian took a turn around the room, ignoring the hotel clerk and his wringing hands. He tugged at the closet door and checked the in-room safe—still closed and locked. Ian punched in his code and thumbed through some cash, a few fake IDs, an airline ticket and his iPod. Everything accounted for and undisturbed.

He then swiveled toward the credenza and cursed. He strode toward it and checked behind the TV, in all the drawers and even beneath a stack of papers. Someone had stolen Kayla's camera.

Crystal groaned and one knot loosened in Ian's gut. At least whoever broke into his room had spared the maid's life. Crystal must not have seen the guy, because if she had, she'd be dead.

Heavy footsteps clumped toward the door again, and Ian looked up to see two uniformed cops clustered around the entryway…and his old friend Sheriff Cahill, hat firmly on his head. Crestville had to be a small town, if the sheriff made an appearance at an assault and robbery.

"Well, whadaya know?" Cahill crossed his arms and puffed out his chest.

"Sheriff." Ian nodded in his direction. "I think the maid has come to."

Ian poked his head into the bathroom. The EMTs had Crystal on the stretcher, an oxygen mask on her face and a bandage on her head.

"Can she talk?" Sheriff Cahill loomed over the group.

"Sure." One of the EMTs removed the mask and Crystal sputtered.

"Who knocked me on the head? One minute I was leaning over cleaning the tub, the next I've got these guys hovering over me with gas masks."

"That's not a gas mask, ma'am." The youngest EMT had a stricken look on his red face. "That's an oxygen mask to help you breathe."

"Well, it's not helping anything."

"So you didn't see who hit you?" Sheriff Cahill took a notebook out of his front pocket.

"No. Didn't hear him either. I propped open the door and was hard at work." She glanced toward the front desk clerk to make sure he'd heard her.

"And what about you, Mr....Shepherd?" Cahill tapped his pencil on the cover of the notebook. "Where were you?"

"I was out. I came back to my room this morning and the cart was down the hall and my door was closed. I discovered her slumped over the tub and called 911."

"Have you had a chance to figure out if anything's missing from your room?" He jabbed the eraser of his pencil in Ian's direction, as if accusing him of something.

Ian shrugged. "Just a camera I foolishly left out on the credenza."

The sheriff narrowed his eyes. "So you think this is a garden variety burglary?"

Crystal protested with a wince of pain. "It's not garden variety to me. We've never had nothing like this happen here before, have we, Tate?"

Tate, the clerk, shook his head so hard his short ponytail whipped from side to side.

"How about it, Mr. Demp…I mean Mr. Shepherd. Garden variety?" Cahill's dark brows formed a straight line over his nose.

Ian shoved his hands in his pockets and wedged his hip against the credenza. "Someone stole a camera. Do you consider that garden variety?"

"Someone bopping a maid on the head to do so has a more sinister ring to it, don't you think?"

"I do."

"How about you, Tate?" Cahill turned to the front desk clerk who'd been following the exchange like a tennis match and now gulped in the face of the sheriff's inquiry.

"Huh?"

Cahill waved his pencil in front of Tate's face. "Did you notice anything suspicious this morning? Anyone ask for Mr. Shepherd here? Did you see anyone lurking around?"

"No, Sheriff Cahill. I knew Crystal was working on this floor, but I didn't hear or see anything."

Cahill had more questions for Crystal and Tate, while Ian pretended to look interested. They didn't know anything, and Cahill knew that.

Ian had a job to do and no time for Cahill's games. He cleared his throat. "Are you guys going to take Crystal to the hospital? She was bleeding and out cold when I found her."

The EMTs answered by strapping Crystal to the stretcher and wheeling her out of the room while she protested loudly. One of the uniformed officers stepped back into the hallway and Cahill spread his arms as if propping up the frame of the door. "You let me know if you find anything else missing."

"I'll do that, Sheriff."

Ian closed the door in Cahill's face, shed his clothing and hopped in the shower. Five minutes later, he yanked on some clean Levis and layered on the rest of his hiking gear…including his weapon.

Time to take a brisk hike along Morningside Trail.

MEG STOPPED FOR the hundredth time that morning to wait for the straggling hikers bringing up the rear. The Rocky Mountain Adventures website and brochure had specifically labeled this hike "easy." And yet, the gently sloping trail, bordered by fall foliage and waving wildflowers, had this bunch huffing and puffing as if scaling K2 in the midst of a snowstorm.

A fake smile stretched across her face as the last of the tourists, a man carrying too much junk, panted toward the group. "Water break?"

Her jolly hikers immediately reached for their packs, fumbling for their water bottles and food. Did she say it was picnic time?

Meg dug the heels of her hands into her eye sockets. *Okay, you had a rough night, but don't take it out on the poor unsuspecting tourists.* How could they possibly know she'd spent a sleepless night in her bed while her husband bunked on the couch in her living room?

Half-naked.

Technically, he'd been wearing jeans, but that still qualified as half-naked. And she'd really enjoyed that half. The two years since he'd retired from Prospero had been kind to his body. His chest still shifted in hard slabs of muscle, his belly a perfect six-pack.

"Meg? Meg?"

"Huh?" She wiped the drool from her chin and turned toward her straggler.

He was studying a sprig of red berries. "Are these safe to eat?"

She extended her hand, wiggling her fingers and he dropped the plant into her palm. She plucked off one of the berries and popped it into her mouth, puckering her lips at the sour taste. "These are okay. But unless you're experienced, you should stick to those granola bars you're chomping on. Safe is sometimes just a few shades darker than poisonous."

The man rubbed his hands on his jeans and plopped down on a large rock, where he proceeded to unpack several items from his pack to pull out a book on Colorado flora and fauna.

He didn't believe her?

Meg chugged some water and then stowed it in her pack. "Are you ready to continue?"

They grumbled a little, but eventually secured their water bottles and lined up on the trail, following her like baby ducks. She glanced over her shoulder, hoping one of those ducks didn't turn out to be a fake. She hadn't wanted to take Ian's advice to stay off the job today, but was relieved she had the easy hike.

At their next lookout point and twenty minutes from the end of the trail, her straggler wailed and dropped his pack to the ground. Meg spun around and stumbled to his side. If she lost another tourist...

"What is it?"

"I left my binoculars back there." He waved his arms

in the direction behind the group, most of who were now rolling their eyes and snickering. *There had to be one in every group.*

With her head still light from the jolt of fear, Meg rubbed her temple. "I'm sorry."

Next time don't bring so much crap.

"I have to go back and get them." He began stuffing his accoutrements back into his pack.

Meg put her hand on his arm. "Oh no, you don't. I can't allow you to go all the way back there on your own."

He glanced up, his eyes owlish behind his glasses. "I can't lose those binoculars. They're not even mine."

"Tell you what." Wrinkling her nose, Meg held up an empty hot water bottle that had fallen out of his backpack. She thrust it into his eager hands and said, "We'll continue the hike as planned, and then if you don't mind waiting about an hour, I'll go back and retrieve your binoculars for you. You can also leave, and I'll just drop them at the office for you to pick up later."

"W-will they still be there?" He shoved the glasses up the bridge of his nose.

"I don't think a fellow hiker would steal your binoculars, unless someone picks them up to turn into our office. And if that's the case, I'll meet them on the trail." She helped him drag the zipper across the bulging backpack. "How does that sound?"

His gaze darted over her shoulder and then back to her face. "I suppose that's okay."

The group behind them gave a collective sigh, and Meg pushed up from the ground to finish her talk and resume the hike. Twenty long, uneventful minutes later, the group looped back to their starting point on the trail and the cars they'd left in the turnout.

The straggler, Evan, retreated to his car while Meg said goodbye to the rest of the group. She strode to Evan's car and he rolled down the window. "It'll take me forty five minutes up and back. Will you be okay here?" She gestured around the empty parking lot, save his car and hers.

"Sure." He patted a cooler on the passenger seat. "I stocked some food in here. Do you want a sandwich?"

"No, thanks. I'm good."

Meg stamped her feet and headed back onto the trail. She could make twice the time without her ducklings trailing behind her.

Although the air had been cold all day, a warm glow had encased her heart whenever she thought about Ian and Travis last night. Travis had always been a friendly baby, but not so touchy-feely as he he'd been with Ian. He instinctively trusted his father.

Meg believed all children intuitively trusted their parents, and continued to do so even after those parents did nothing to warrant that trust. That's why parents like Ian's devastated children—devastated Ian.

They'd both been drunks, and when a baby had come along, they'd had no clue what to do with him. Who knows if Ian would've been better off in the System. His parents always kept one step ahead of social services.

Ian had learned survival skills the hard way. When he graduated from high school, he enlisted in the army and took on every challenge they threw at him with vigor and commitment. He had something to prove.

He'd probably exhibit that same commitment toward his son, again yearning to prove to himself that his birth was simply an accident of genes.

Meg almost growled when she spotted the silver wrapper of a granola bar in the middle of the trail. She hoped someone had dropped that accidentally, since she'd always felt a twinge of guilt leading people into this pristine wilderness. Of course, if she didn't do it somebody else would, and then she'd have no control at all.

She'd almost reached the spot where Evan left his binoculars, and hadn't run across anyone else. They should be right where he left them. Meg pumped her legs harder, faster, stronger, to get there. She rounded the curve of the trail and tripped over the toes of her boots.

A tall man had the binoculars to his eyes and was scanning the gorge that fell off to the right. But he was no ordinary tourist on a solitary hike.

Ian lowered the binoculars and smiled.

Meg's silly heart sang like a bird obliviously flying straight toward a plateglass window. She smiled back anyway, bracing for the impact.

"What are you doing in these parts?"

"Bird watching." Ian raised the binoculars hitched around his neck, and then let them drop where they thudded against his chest.

"You followed me." She tried for an accusatory tone, but it came out all sticky sweet and melting.

"I hit the trail shortly after you and your group did, and kept you in my sights. Wasn't hard—slowest bunch of hikers I ever encountered."

Meg grimaced. "You and me both, and then one of them left his binoculars behind. Care to tell me the purpose of your exercise?"

She already knew, but she wanted to hear him say it. Maybe it would wipe clean his other statement last night about how he wasn't the least bit interested in sharing her bed. She wanted to shake the sand over that one, clearing the Etch-a-Sketch for sweeter sentiments.

"You know I didn't want you going on this hike." He shrugged, the puffy shoulders of his down vest reaching his earlobes. "When I realized you didn't give a damn about my wants, I figured I could keep tabs on you anyway."

Oh, she gave a damn about his wants. Every last one of them.

"That's honorable of you, but completely unnecessary. Did you have a chance to do any more digging on those tourists?"

"No, but something else happened." He skimmed his fingers along the straps of the binoculars.

His tight jaw caused her heart to do a little dance. The something else that happened couldn't possibly be a lottery win or the discovery that his drunken parents kidnapped him from the Cleaver family.

"Just spit it out, Dempsey."

"When I got back to my hotel room this morning, the maid was out cold and someone had tossed the room and stolen Kayla's camera."

She gasped, bringing her hands to her mouth. "Is she okay, the maid?"

"She has a big lump on her head, but she's lucky."

"Lucky?"

"Lucky she didn't see the guy."

A chill brushed across her flesh. "And what about Kayla's camera? Wasn't it broken?"

"I checked it when I got back to the room and it was in working order again. I clicked through the pictures and was planning to enlarge them. Someone took a shot of her right before she died…probably her killer."

The chill deepened and Meg hugged herself. First her place and then Ian's hotel room. This guy had a line on them. Why didn't he just try to find the suitcase himself? Did he think they had something he wanted?

Ian grabbed her gloved hands. "Are you cold?"

"To the bone."

"I have an idea. Are you in a hurry?" His green eyes flashed with a challenge and an edge of mischief. How many times had she seen that look in Travis's eyes?

He still had her hands in a warm clasp, and he increased the pressure on her fingers, as if to sway her. All he had to do was take her in his arms, press those soft lips against hers and she'd follow him anywhere.

"Well, I do have to take those binoculars you've appropriated back to their rightful owner."

"His fault for leaving them."

"What's your plan?"

He pointed to the ridge across the gorge. "Aren't the falls around that bend?"

"Yeah."

"Kayla would've had a clear view of that area from where she was standing. Once we went down to the river, we lost that perspective."

"Are you suggesting we hike down there and have a look?" She bit her lip, holding her breath. Another adventure with Ian? It had been too long and too lonely.

"It shouldn't take long. It's just the two of us. You're not leading a bunch of whiny tourists."

Just the two of us. And Travis.

"Why not? If Evan really wants his binoculars, he can pick them up at the office…or report me missing with stolen property."

They drank some water and then began their descent into the thick, green carpet spiked with toffee-colored streaks and bursts of amber, purple, red-gold and sunset orange—the tapestry of autumn in the Rocky Mountains.

They cut a swath through the dense vegetation, creating their own trail that no other human could follow. Meg inhaled the strong scent of pine and it cleared her mind, stripping her senses clean. The wilderness saved her when Ian left, when her marriage had failed. It had steadily renewed her faith in everything, including herself. It had always been her refuge.

Especially when her mother and twin sister died. Meg would've been in that limo when the drunken limo driver smashed it into a cement bridge, if she had followed the plan her father had laid out for her and her twin, Kate. He'd wanted both of them to follow the society girl route, but only Meg refused him. Kate had agreed to the whole debutante mess to garner their father's love and approval. Kate and Mom had been on their way home from one of those stupid balls.

And her father had never been able to disguise the fact that he wished Meg had been in that car instead of Kate. Kate, the one who'd given up control of her own life just to see a little approval in their father's cold face. Meg would never give up control—ever.

She blinked her eyes and zeroed-in on Ian's back. He'd almost reached the bottom.

Ian jumped into a clearing, planting his boots firmly on the ground. He held out his arms to her. "Ready?"

The branch Meg held in her grip slipped from her grasp and she flung herself against Ian's chest. She hit him square in the solar plexus and he tumbled backward with a grunt.

"Whoa." He cushioned her fall by placing his body between her and the hard ground.

"Are you okay?" She braced herself with her arms

on either side of his body, puffing a cold breath into his face.

Blinking, he tightened his arms around her, backpack and all. "I didn't think you were going to throw yourself down the rest of the incline. I wasn't ready for you."

She blew upward at a piece of her bangs hanging in her eyes. "I'm sorry. I lost my grip."

And her concentration.

"No harm done." He slipped his hands beneath her pack, splaying his fingers across her lower back. "You're as light as a puff of dandelion."

"Is that why you grunted when I took you down?"

He grinned. "I always grunt when I'm having a good time. Don't you remember?"

She had a hard time forgetting, even when she wanted to. And she didn't want to right now. She could depend on Ian without getting swallowed up. He'd been as skittish as she was when it came to making commitments. It had suited them both...once. Meg moistened her lips with the tip of her tongue, her face inches from his.

He moved his hand from her back to the nape of her neck. He nudged her head forward with his long fingers, plowing through her hair.

She closed her eyes when their lips met, but a burst of light exploded behind her lids. Sunshine poured into all the dark recesses of her soul, warming her, nourishing her. She kissed him back, opening her mouth slightly, feeling her way back into his heart with tentative steps. One false move and he might remember she'd kept Travis from him for two years. Then he'd end the magic of their kiss.

Ian kept possession of her mouth while slipping the straps of her backpack from her shoulders and shoving it off her body. His hands burrowed beneath her layers of clothing to find the warm skin of her back. His gloved finger traced the line of her spine and she shivered from anticipation more than the cold touch of his glove.

He smiled against her lips. "If you're cold, I'm not doing my job."

Before she could assure him that a blazing heat had invaded every cell of her body, he rolled her onto her back and nudged her onto a dense carpet of soft grass. Straddling her, he shrugged off his own backpack and then buried his head against her neck.

She had no idea what they hoped to accomplish on a chilly afternoon at the bottom of a gorge with fifty layers of clothing between each other's bare skin. But right now she couldn't think beyond the soft lips and sharp teeth that alternately kissed and nibbled at her flesh.

Ian swirled his tongue in the hollow of her throat, and Meg moaned, skimming one hand through his cropped hair and flinging the other to her side in wild abandon to the sensation. He trailed his tongue lower. She curled the fingers of her outstretched hand and froze.

Ian murmured against her chest. "Do you want me to stop?"

She jerked her hand back and twisted her head to the side. Gasping, she wrapped both arms around Ian in a vice grip.

"I think we just found Hans."

Chapter Nine

Ian stopped his sweet journey down Meg's body and whipped his head around. His gaze followed the direction of her shaking finger to a white hand curled into a fist and sprinkled with dark hair. Instinctively, he pulled Meg away from the arm that beckoned from the underbrush.

Rolling off her body, he yanked her into a sitting position almost in his lap. "How do you know it's Hans? It could be someone else."

"There's nobody else missing in these mountains, Ian."

"Not that we're aware of, anyway. Maybe someone jumped out of that plane along with the suitcase." He and the colonel had considered that possibility. They'd considered all possibilities.

"I don't know which prospect is worse." She slid from his lap and crawled toward the body. "But don't you think we'd better find out?"

"Let me." He grabbed her ankle, his fingers wrapping around the thick leather of her hiking boot.

Digging her knees into the mulch, she glanced over her shoulder. "We'll do it together."

Ian nodded. He hadn't married a girly-girl. He shuffled

on his knees beside her and bent forward, sweeping back the foliage that obscured the upper torso of the body.

The man's pack lay beside him, wrenched from his back, and wet leaves covered his face. Ian said a small prayer that the animals hadn't gotten to his flesh yet. Meg may not be a girly-girl, but she didn't need that vision burned into her brain.

"Are you ready?" His hand hovered over the man's face. "You can look away."

"Uh, maybe I will. I can already tell you it's Hans. I recognize his backpack. I don't need to see his face... or what might be left of it."

Meg turned her head into Ian's shoulder while he brushed the leaves from Hans's head. He blew out a breath, plucking one last twig from the man's intact face. "Nothing got to him yet, and you're right. This is Hans Birnbacher."

"Birnbacher? That's his last name?"

"That's the name he used to book the hike. My CIA contact checked him out and he came back clean, but we still don't know if that name is a cover or the real thing."

Meg gestured to Hans's lifeless form. "What do you think now? Real or Memorex?"

Ian shuffled in closer to the body and checked the man's pulse against his ice cold throat. Nothing there. "If he was involved with the arms dealers or the terrorists, he must've stepped on some toes."

"Stepped on toes? That's a polite way to put it. You don't have to dress it up for me, Ian."

"And if he wasn't involved with either of them, he must've *really* screwed up—big-time case of wrong universe, wrong century." Ian didn't want to move the body, but he didn't have a clue how Hans had died. If he'd taken a bullet to the back of the head, it hadn't made its way through the front. Hans had on too many clothes for Ian to tell whether or not someone had shot his torso.

Meg sat back on her heels and fumbled with the radio in her pocket. "He was a curious guy on the hike, always asking about this or that. Sometimes asking questions totally unrelated to the mountains. Maybe he asked someone the wrong question."

"Are you going to call it in?" He pointed to the radio in her hand. Sheriff Cahill would have a field day with this one. He just might run Ian out of town on a rail.

"What do you suggest?" She tilted the radio back and forth. "We just leave him here to rot?"

"Of course not. Just wish I had a better handle on his identity." Ian pushed to his feet and dragged the binoculars from his backpack. With a sweeping motion, he surveyed the terrain across the gorge. "What do you think Hans was doing out here?"

Turning, he focused the lenses on the wooden lookout beyond the waterfall. Kayla had a clear view of this gorge before she died. Did Hans see something, too? Did he return on his own to check it out?

A twig snapped and Ian jerked, banging the binoculars against the bridge of his nose. "What was that?"

"Little jumpy?" Meg stood up, brushing debris from her clothing with one hand and clutching the radio in the other.

"Anyone who takes a picture of this gorge or ventures into it turns to stone or winds up dead. Hell, yes, I'm jumpy."

"Well, that was an animal."

"So was whatever did that to him." He pointed to Hans, who could tell no secrets now.

Meg got on the radio and gave their coordinates to

the mountain rescue team. She slipped the radio in her vest pocket. "They want us to wait with the body."

"Did they ask what you were doing here?"

"Not yet, but then I work here. What's your excuse?"

"I'm with you." He jerked his thumb toward her.

"You know, it's a good thing that maid survived the attack in your room this morning, or you'd have three deaths at your doorstep."

"Cahill doesn't like me."

She waved her hands. "Pete doesn't like anyone."

"Anyone close to you?"

"He's a little protective."

"And a little smitten."

"Pete doesn't get smitten by anything or anyone." She turned her back on Hans and paced away from him. "We're just friends. He's been good to Travis."

That twisted the knife. "I'm glad. I'll have to thank him for it one day." Ian clamped down on the wave of jealousy that threatened to make a fool out of him. He coughed and cleared his throat. "So what do you think about Hans? Innocent tourist or unlucky terrorist?"

Meg scuffed the toe of her boot against the dirt. "When he first disappeared, I had a hard time believing he'd killed Kayla. I may not be the greatest judge of character, but he seemed like a standard, if overly enthusiastic, tourist."

Ian's head snapped up. Had she directed that last comment at him? Was she implying she'd misjudged his character when they got married? He smacked his cold hands together and stamped his feet.

He had to stop thinking about Meg at every turn, when he should be focused on this case. Just his luck the terrorists had dumped their cargo in Meg's neck of the woods. Even though his presence here led to the discovery of his son, surely there could've been a better time to find out about Travis. Would Meg have even attempted to contact him if he hadn't crash-landed on her mountain?

Red-hot flames of anger leaped in his belly every time he thought about her deception. Okay, maybe avoidance rang truer than deception, but it engendered the same emotion. He wanted to stay angry at her, but her voice, her touch, her smell sent different kinds of red-hot flames to his belly.

The thwack of the helicopter blades cut through his tangled thinking. Shading his eyes, he looked to the sky. The big bird blotted out the sun and then dipped and weaved to find a safe spot to land.

Meg waved her arms overhead. "I think they brought an EMT with them. Maybe he can give us Hans's cause of death."

"This is going to be a crime scene now." Ian tracked the binoculars along the slopes and crags of the gorge. "There's something here, Meg. I can feel it. Something has invaded this peaceful place and has left an ugly mark."

She tilted her head as she watched the chopper touch down. "There have been two murders here, Ian. That's evil enough. I'm not convinced there's anything special about this place. I don't see any suitcase or weapon, do you?"

"Not yet, but it's here. I'm sure of it."

"Then we need to find it first." She swung around as the mountain rescue team hopped out of the helicopter.

One of the rescue team recognized Ian from the day before, but they'd all been briefed as to Ian's true identity, and nothing seemed to surprise these guys.

Ian led them to the body, which was still tucked

beneath the bush where they'd found him. "I didn't move him, except to brush the leaves from his face to ID him. He's the missing tourist from yesterday."

The EMT bringing up the rear barked, "Cause of death?"

"I thought you could tell me. Like I said, I didn't want to touch him." Ian faced Meg and rolled his eyes.

The EMT Meg had called Greg crouched beside Hans. "Do we have a serial killer on our hands out here, Meg?"

Twining her fingers together, she shot a sideways glance at Ian. "Define serial killer."

"Really?" He twisted his head to the side and raised his brows. "Dead body yesterday, dead body today. I'd say that's a good definition."

"It's not like every tourist in Crestville has something to fear."

"Just the ones along these particular trails. I talked to Sheriff Cahill after we got your call. He's thinking of shutting down the trails out here."

Ian nodded. "That's not a bad idea. Would Rocky Mountain Adventures lose a lot of money?"

"The season is winding to a close anyway. Once the snow gets here, more tourists are interested in the skiing than the hiking, mountaineering or rock climbing." Meg gazed up at the gray clouds scattered across the misty sky, her cheeks red with the cold. "And the snow is on its way."

The EMT yanked off his gloves. "His neck is broken."

"Accident or intentional?" Ian hunched his shoulders and tightened his abs, as if ready to take a punch. He already knew the answer, even if the clueless EMT didn't.

"I don't know." The EMT matched Ian's shrug. "He could've broken it in a fall."

Ian let his gaze wander from Hans's inert form, across the rugged terrain and then up the tree- and shrub-dotted hillside he and Meg had traversed earlier. A fall? Not bloody likely.

"Any marks or bruises on his neck?" Ian knew how to snap a man's neck with his bare hands. He figured any well-trained operative worth his salt could do the same.

Spinning in a circle, the EMT flapped his arms. "Does this look like an examination room to you? An autopsy can tell us more."

Ian cocked an eyebrow at Meg. *Not if this guy was performing it.* "Is Sheriff Cahill on his way to search the area?"

Greg stepped forward. "We have orders not to move the body until he gets here."

Another chopper swooped into the valley, announcing Cahill's arrival. In two steps, Ian was beside Meg. He moved his lips close to her ear. "This should be interesting."

"Try not to antagonize him and things will go a lot more smoothly."

He snorted. "Who said I wanted things to go smoothly?"

Cahill had his job to do and Ian had his. Those jobs might bisect along the way, but Ian had no intention of bringing the sheriff into a top-secret investigation. Ian wouldn't be responsible for putting Jack's life in any more danger.

Cahill dropped from the chopper and, once clear of the blades and the wind they stirred up, sauntered toward the group hovering around Hans's body. *Swaggered* would be a better word. He acted like he owned this mountain...and Meg.

Ian squared his shoulders and dug the heels of his hiking boots into the cold earth. For now, this mountain belonged to him. And Meg? He wrenched his mind away from thoughts of Meg and her warm, pliant body...and her cold, deceiving heart. He'd sort that out another time, when Cahill's gaze wasn't drilling him.

The sheriff brushed past Ian, tipped his hat at Meg and crouched beside the body. "Well, whaddya know? Mr. Covert Ops here decides to take another hike and another dead body turns up."

"Technically, this one was already here when I arrived."

Cahill ignored him and pushed to his feet. "Meg? What were you doing out here this late? I thought you were leading the Morningside hike, and that should've ended over an hour ago."

Ian clenched his jaw. Did the guy keep track of Meg's schedule? The fact not only annoyed the hell out of Ian, it should be creeping-out Meg.

He glanced at her smiling up at the sheriff, her eyes bright and her cheeks glowing. She didn't look creeped-out in the least.

"I was and it did, Pete, but one of the hikers left his binoculars, so I came back for them. I ran into Ian, and we decided to take a look around."

Cahill leveled a finger at Ian. "I'd stay as far away from this guy as you can, Meg. Trouble follows him like groupies tail a rock star."

At Cahill's ridiculous analogy, Ian covered a smirk with his hand and then turned it into a yawn when Cahill switched his attention from Meg to him.

Meg's lips twitched. "He has a job to do, Pete, just

like you. Now, is this officially a crime scene? Because the guys from mountain rescue have been trampling all over the place."

"And you two?" He swept an arm to encompass Meg and Ian. "Have you been trampling all over the place looking for clues?"

"We didn't want to disturb a crime scene, Sheriff. I didn't even move the body when we found it. Still don't know the exact cause of death." He tilted his head toward the EMT now mucking with a clipboard.

The EMT looked up and shoved his glasses up his nose. "I told you the victim broke his neck."

"But you haven't determined whether an accident or a person broke his neck."

"The coroner will determine that." Cahill turned his shoulder to Ian and faced Meg. "My deputies and I will be out here for a while. You can get a ride with the sheriff's department helicopter. You, too, Dempsey."

"That's okay, Sheriff. I started a hike this morning and I'm going to finish it." Ian said the words to Cahill's back without even looking at Meg. He figured this was a test for her: him or Cahill.

"I wouldn't feel right leaving Ian here all by himself. I don't want to lose another visitor in these mountains."

She'd chosen him. A flush of victory washed over Ian and he felt like a ten-year-old boy on the school yard.

Cahill snorted. "I don't think Dempsey needs a tour guide, Meg. Just be careful. We'll be here for a while, if you need any help."

As Cahill scattered orders among the deputies and EMTs, Ian and Meg zigzagged away from the scene of the crime, plunging deeper into the gorge.

When they'd trekked out of eyesight and earshot, Ian grabbed Meg around the waist and pulled her backward.

"That puffed-up sheriff had one thing right. You do need to be careful."

She turned in his arms and looked into his face. "If Hans is the one who killed Kayla, what happened to Hans?"

"We don't know for sure if Hans did kill Kayla. Maybe he saw what she saw and someone took him out, too. So far, all of the people on that hike have checked out, including Hans. We need to concentrate on finding that suitcase."

Her wide eyes scanned the gorge that tumbled out before them in the hodgepodged chaos of nature. "It's like looking for a needle in a haystack."

He nodded. "That's what I'm thinking, but Kayla must've been close to something. Hans, too. And I think this area is key."

Meg's radio crackled and they both jumped. She stepped back and yanked it out of her pocket.

"Meg, where are you? We heard you found the German tourist's body?"

"I'm hiking back in, Matt."

"Why didn't you take Pete's chopper?"

"Just wanted a look around." She met Ian's eyes and shrugged.

Meg always did catch on quickly.

"There's a man here looking for his binoculars."

Meg covered her mouth and snorted. "I have them. Tell Evan to come back to the office tomorrow to pick them up, or better yet, I'll drop them off at his hotel tonight."

"Meg…"

"Over and out, Matt." She stowed the radio in her pack and clapped her hands together. "Okay, let's get down to business."

"We need to find that case. If Kayla, and possibly Hans, saw it, we can, too."

"It's not going to blow up in our faces when we find it, is it?"

"If it survived a drop from an airplane, I doubt we have to worry about that." He brushed strawberry-blond bangs from her eyes. "You don't need to do this, Meg."

Her eyelashes swept across her eyes, extinguishing the blue blaze that flared momentarily. "Don't shut me out, Ian. I know I don't deserve your trust, or even your friendship, after keeping Travis from you."

She stopped and Ian zipped his lips, not wanting to contradict her. Did he forgive her? Did he understand her reasons? He knew all too well why she'd done it. He hadn't exactly popped the champagne when Meg had announced her first pregnancy. The news filled him with doubts and fears. He hadn't had time to grow accustomed to the idea of fatherhood because Meg miscarried eight weeks into the pregnancy.

When he'd tried to comfort her, she'd accused him of being insincere and relieved that he didn't have to step up and be a parent. He hadn't felt relief, not at all. The loss of their baby had gouged another hole in his battered heart. It had spurred on his panic that he couldn't keep a child safe—even before he made it into the world.

He couldn't put those feelings into words, so Meg couldn't offer him the solace he'd needed. He burrowed further into work, and she withdrew. The beginning of the end of their marriage.

"I don't want to shut you out, Meg." He traced the delicate line of her jaw with his thumb. "Ever again."

"Good. I don't want that either." She grabbed his hand. "So let me help you. This is my territory. I know this landscape better than any guide at Rocky Mountain.

If anyone's going to find some obscure suitcase in the wild, it's going to be me."

"Okay." He pointed toward the lookout where Kayla had been standing. "What area could she have seen from up there? And could Hans have been heading toward the same place?"

Meg bit her lip and squinted as she peered at the wooden platform, yellow tape now flapping from the railings to warn people away. "Your initial observation was correct. If Kayla was facing away from the falls, she would've had a clear view of this area. We took the hard way down today. Hans could've backtracked on the trail and followed another path leading down to this same spot. But why? If he's an innocent bystander, why would he take the time and trouble to come down here?"

Ian twisted the cap off his bottle of water and chugged the remainder. "Someone looking for this weapon is on the hike. He notices Kayla zeroing-in on something. Maybe he already has his suspicions about her or me. He pushes her over. Hans witnesses everything and thinks maybe there's money to be had, or plans some kind of blackmail. When Hans disappears from the hike, our man goes after him and kills him, too."

"That's your theory?" She drew her brows together. "What if Hans is the one who killed Kayla, and he traipses down here to look for whatever she saw and winds up with a broken neck from a fall?"

"That works, too. In fact, I like yours better, because that means there wasn't another tourist on your hike who isn't what he pretended to be. I was supposed to be going over the names of the people on your hike yesterday."

"Instead, you followed me on my hike."

He tugged on a lock of her silky hair. "I'm not going

to allow you to be out here on your own, Meg-o. So you can go ahead and lead as many hikes as you like, but you're going to have a shadow."

"I'm beginning to think Pete was right." Her lip quirked up on one side when she noticed his clenched hands. "I mean, when he suggested we suspend operations for a while, maybe the rest of the season. The skiers are going to be showing up in droves after the first snowfall, and there's no way we can keep people out then."

Smiling, Ian flexed his fingers. "Okay, I admit he's right...about that. How's Matt going to feel about suspending his business?"

"Matt's not going to be happy. Business hasn't been great. We used to lead rafting trips on the Hawkins River, but we had to stop those because we didn't get a lot of bookings. I don't think Matt's the best businessman out there. He never wants to spend a cent on promo or advertising."

"I'm not sure Sheriff Cahill can force Matt to close his operations on the mountain, so it might be up to Matt in the end." He held up Evan's binoculars. "Are you ready to do some searching? You're not going to be late picking up Travis or anything, are you?"

"No. I'm still on the job. I'm supposed to be doing paperwork in the office." She winked. "Guess Matt isn't the only lousy businessperson."

THEY CANVASSED THE AREA in grids, and the crisp, cold air gave Ian a heightened sense of awareness. He could feel it in the way the adrenaline zinged through his blood, in the way everything had a sharp, clean focus—discovery lay just within their grasp.

A bevy of birds took flight from a tree to Meg's left and a rabbit scurried across his path, almost running across his boots. The creatures didn't appreciate their intrusion. Probably wondering why the heck these annoying humans didn't stay on their own trails.

He and Meg wended their way back toward each other as they headed into the next grid. Ian raised his head from studying the ground to give Meg a smile and an encouraging pat when they crossed paths.

Sensing his regard, she jerked her head up and almost simultaneously caught her foot on a root coming up from the ground. She tripped forward, giving a squeal and flinging up her arms. The squeal turned to a cry and a look of terror twisted her features.

Then Meg fell to the ground, blissfully, safely out of range of the gun now pointing at Ian.

Chapter Ten

The whiz of the bullet sailing past Meg's ear reverberated like a swarm of angry hornets. She hit the ground, a blaze of heat burning her right shoulder. Since she'd thrown her hands up instead of out, her chest and stomach took the full impact of the fall, still hard despite a bed of pine needles.

Upon landing, she lifted her head, scraping her chin. Ian tumbled to the ground himself, his mouth wide but emitting no sound or maybe Meg just couldn't hear him over the roaring in her ears.

Oh God, if Ian had been shot, she'd track down his killer and make him pay. She'd even grovel for her father to use his influence to do it. When the air gushed back into her lungs, she screamed, "Ian."

He bunched up to his knees and launched himself at her, falling on top of her body. He already had his weapon clutched in his hand, and he swung it around in one smooth movement and squeezed off two shots.

Meg's racing heart had her gasping for breath. The shooter must still be within range. Using his body as a shield, Ian scooted toward an elderberry bush, dragging Meg's body beneath his. Once he had them both behind the generous growth of the bush, he hunched up to his elbows and took aim again.

The blast from Ian's gun deafened Meg and she squeezed her eyes shut, her nostrils flaring at the acrid scent of the gunpowder. Ian shifted, creating a slice of space between their bodies, and Meg huddled against him, sealing her throbbing shoulder against his.

She opened one eye and peered through the mass of leaves, holding her breath, fearful one small puff from her lips could initiate another exchange of gunfire. Ian's finger curled around the trigger of his gun. The tense muscles of his body, coiled and ready for action, pressed against Meg. Every fiber of the man vibrated with deadly intent.

Something or someone crashed through the underbrush behind them. Ian rolled onto his back, leveling his weapon in front of him. The crackling of twigs and dislodging of rocks continued, but faded, as Meg strained her ears and squinted into the wild growth that seemed to suck up the sound.

Ian's low voice next to her ear sounded like a shout. "I think he's gone."

Meg swallowed, her throat too dry to speak. She scratched out a few unintelligible words and then grabbed her aching shoulder. Her fingers met a wet spot soaking through torn bits of her jacket. She pulled her hand away and stared at the red streaks on her palm. After the fast and furious few minutes of terror, her mind now seemed as slow as a river of sludge.

She stared at her hand, wiggling her fingers and clenching her fist. Nothing injured or broken.

"Meg!" Ian grabbed her wrist. "You're hurt. God, where did he hit you?"

"Hit me?" She knitted her brows and bit her lip until the pain in her shoulder blazed to life again. She gasped. "My shoulder."

Ian crawled around to her other side and cursed. He unzipped her jacket and yanked it from her good arm. Then he carefully peeled it from her injured one.

Her flannel shirt beneath her jacket and her silk long underwear beneath the shirt both sported jagged tears. Ian hooked his fingers into the holes and ripped a wider circle around her wound.

Blood trickled down her arm and Meg gulped. "Is it bad? I don't feel faint or anything, just hurts like the blazes."

"The bullet didn't lodge in your arm." Ian snatched the water bottle from the side of his pack and pulled a T-shirt from the main compartment. He ripped the T-shirt in half and soaked one piece.

"Does this hurt?" He dabbed at her shoulder and she gritted her teeth.

"Not much."

He cleaned the blood from her arm, took the other piece of the torn T-shirt and pressed it against the injury. "Thank God, the bullet just grazed you. I think you tripped just about the same time he got off his shot."

Sitting back down, Ian dragged Meg between his legs, her back against his chest. He continued to apply pressure to the bullet wound and held a bottle of water to her lips. "Drink. Do you feel dizzy?"

"I feel shocked, but it's emotional, not physical. Do you think he was tracking us or lying in wait?"

He brushed his lips against her hair. "Let's not talk about it right now."

Ian was back to sweeping unpleasant things under the rug, protecting her, keeping her in the dark. "He might still be out there waiting for us."

"I don't think so. If he didn't know I was armed before, he does now. That's going to give him a healthy dose of caution." He removed the bunched-up T-shirt from her shoulder, inspected it and began wrapping the shirt around her upper arm. "You stopped bleeding already. It's really nothing much more than a scrape. Do you have some ibuprofen in your pack?"

She tapped the toe of her boot against the outside pocket of her backpack. "In there. If this is the spot and the guy knows what he's looking for, why doesn't he just grab it and run? Why is he still in the area? Why is he killing anyone getting close?"

"All good questions." Ian helped her back into her jacket. Then he reached around her for the pack and removed the bottle of ibuprofen. "And I don't have the answer to any of them."

He popped the lid on the bottle and shook two green gel caps into his palm. "I think a flesh wound from a bullet calls for two, don't you?"

She tossed the pills into her mouth and chugged some water. "How about ten?"

Immediately his brows created a V over his nose. "Are you in a lot of pain?"

"On a scale of one to ten? About a seven."

He patted her breast, and just when she was getting some ideas, he pulled the radio out of her jacket pocket. "Do you suppose your good friend, Sheriff Cahill, is still in the area with his chopper?"

She blinked. "You're going to ask for his help? I thought you'd be willing to burn in hell first."

"Don't be dense, Meg." He tapped her nose with the radio antenna. "I'd be willing to burn in hell first, but I'm not about to let you burn in hell with me. There's no way you're walking out of this valley with that injury."

Ian said, "Call him." He dropped the radio in her lap and she got the sheriff's department helicopter on her frequency. She explained everything to the pilot, who told her the deputies weren't done with the Hans crime scene yet. Meg welcomed the news, since the pilot agreed to pick up her and Ian, while leaving the deputies to their investigation on the ground. She couldn't deal with any more male posturing between Ian and Pete right now.

"The pilot's on his way."

"I heard everything. Cahill's going to have another investigation on his hands with this shooting."

Meg snuggled against Ian's chest and draped one arm over his thigh while holding the other close to her body. "Why don't you just tell him everything and get law enforcement out here to search?"

"Nope." He balanced his chin on her head and shook his head. "This kind of operation is done undercover, only by those in the know, and away from the glare of the media. We don't even know what we're after here. A full-scale search could jeopardize the mission, law enforcement lives and Jack's safety. I'll tell Cahill what he needs to know to do his job, no more."

"That's why Pete is…uh…annoyed with you. He doesn't like being shut out." *Any more than I do.*

"Pete isn't annoyed with me. He hates me, and his dislike doesn't have anything to do with this case."

Warmth crawled across Meg's cheeks. "He doesn't have dibs on me, Ian. Nobody does."

"You're wrong."

Her blood pounded in her veins, and the wound beneath Ian's tight dressing throbbed. Would he admit it now? Her discovery of Hans's body had interrupted their kisses. The gunfire had intruded upon their companionable hike. Could Ian get past her deception?

She waited, her gloved fingers curled like claws on his knee.

His warm breath stirred her hair. "Travis has dibs on you. He has your heart and soul."

The tight muscles of her face dissolved into a huge smile and she scuffed her glove against Ian's thigh. "You noticed?"

"Hard to miss that between a mother and child."

His words had a harsh edge, and Meg finished his sentence in her head: *Even if you've never experienced it yourself.*

She cranked her head to the side and kissed the edge of his stubbled chin. "I'm glad you can see that. I'm glad I didn't make a mess of things…even though I made the biggest mistake of my life in not telling you about the pregnancy."

"That's why I need to keep you out of harm's way, Meg. You need to be there for Travis."

And you, Ian? Do I need to be there for you, too?

The helicopter appeared above the tree line and Ian jumped to his feet, waving his arms. He hooked an arm beneath Meg's good shoulder and helped her to her feet. "You're going to have to walk a little, since he can't put his bird down here."

"Nothing wrong with my legs."

He aimed a glance at the weapon clutched in his hand. "I've got your back."

Once on her feet, she stumbled against him. "Great. I hadn't thought of the shooter out there, ready to take pot shots at us while we're making our escape."

"This is just insurance. He's long gone. He's not going to take any chances with a helicopter hovering nearby."

As the plane set down and they quickly hopped on,

Meg's gaze skittered toward the dense foliage where the shooter had scurried like a cockroach exposed to the light. "You keep that insurance close by and ready to deliver."

The chopper lifted off and dipped to the right, almost skimming the tops of the ponderosa pines still dressed in green and awaiting winter. Meg rested her forehead against the helicopter's window and the scenery melted into blurry lines beneath her.

Where was the suitcase? Where was the killer? And what had happened to her peaceful wonderland?

IAN DROVE HER to the hospital, the same one Travis had visited the day before. The doctor pronounced her first gunshot wound ever a superficial flesh wound, cleaned it, dressed it and called the police.

Of course, the police in Crestville meant one of Pete's deputies, who explained that Pete was still tied up with the investigation of the dead tourist.

Meg recounted to him how she and Ian had decided to hike out of the valley after discovering Hans Birnbach's body, and somebody took a shot at them.

Ian said, with a completely straight face, "Do you get many poachers? It could've been someone on an early hunting trip."

Pete must've briefed all of his deputies on the covert ops military man in their midst. This one narrowed his eyes and snorted. "After two deaths already? I don't think so, Dempsey."

Ian raised his hands and shrugged. "Can Meg leave now? She has to pick up…her son."

Meg hadn't even bothered returning to the Rocky Mountain Adventures office. She didn't have any time to do anything but pick up Travis and get ready for a dinner party she'd already planned.

Outside of the hospital, Ian raked his nails across his short hair. "You're throwing a dinner party with a bum shoulder? You need rest."

"You heard the doc—superficial flesh wound. It's not like I'm going to cook. I'll pick up some take-out Chinese. It's a casual dinner with the parents of Travis's friends, and the kids are invited."

"I don't think you should be alone tonight, Meg. Someone just tried to shoot you." He folded his arms, blocking her way to the parking lot.

"Didn't you hear me? I'm having a bunch of people over. I won't be alone."

"Any one of those people going to spend the night?"

"Of course not." She pushed past him, making a bee-line for his rental car. He beeped the remote before she got to the passenger door, so she opened it and slipped onto the seat, slamming the door behind her.

He climbed in next to her, the economy car too small for his large frame. She pushed the hair out of her face and collapsed against the seat, closing her eyes. "Couldn't the CIA or the government, or whoever, spring for a bigger car?"

"Don't want to waste the taxpayers' money." He cranked on the engine and pulled out of the parking space. When he rolled over a speed bump, Meg grabbed her elbow in the sling.

He sucked air in through his teeth. "Sorry about that. You're still going to host a dinner party?"

"You make it sound like an official White House function or something. It's just a bunch of parents getting together with their kids—paper plates, sippy cups and talk of potty training strategies."

"How's Travis doing with that, anyway?"

She opened one eyelid to study his profile—still strong, clean, chiseled…and serious. He really wanted to know about Travis's progress. And she owed it to him. She scooped in a breath and straightened in her seat. "Boys are generally slower in that area than girls, so I'm not going to start with him until he's two and a half. I don't want to set him up for failure."

A muscle flared in his jaw. "No, don't ever do that."

Ian's stiff expression opened a floodgate for Meg. All the way to Travis's day care, she talked about their son. She told Ian about his birth and his personality and all his firsts. All the firsts Ian had missed because of her stubborn pride.

When they pulled in front of Eloise's house, Ian knew a lot more about Travis than when he'd left him that morning. His questions had spurred on Meg to tell even more stories about Travis. Sure, she had friends who cared about Travis, but Meg had never had anyone to talk to about him in this intimate way. And Ian had welcomed it, devoured every word she said with a seemingly insatiable hunger.

He parked the car and then smacked the steering wheel. "Do you think Eloise will have an extra car seat? I'm going to take both of you home instead of to your car. You still don't have great range of motion, and shouldn't be driving."

"Are you sure?" She lifted her arm, bound by the sling, and winced. "Okay. Good idea."

"D-do you want to come in with me?" She clenched the handle of the door, afraid he'd say no.

"Yep." Ian pushed out of the car and strode around

to her side and helped her out of the seat as if she were made out of fine crystal.

She shrugged him off with her good arm. "Don't forget the walker in the back."

He ignored her, taking possession of her arm again and walking up to Eloise's house beside her, with slow, measured steps. The loss of blood had made her a little woozy in the ER, but she felt almost normal now. Her gunshot wound was a dull ache instead of a raging fire on her upper arm.

When Eloise opened the door, she brought her hand to her mouth. "What happened?"

"It's a long story, Eloise. I had an accident on one of the hikes, but I'm fine. Did Travis have a good day?"

Ian hung by the door, but Eloise sized him up with an appraising look. "Felicia told me Travis's father had come to town."

"That's right." Ian stepped around Meg and extended his hand. "Ian Dempsey."

"I'm Eloise Zinn. Travis is a wonderful boy." She motioned them to the back of the house, and Meg watched Travis scribbling chalk on a blackboard.

Sensing their presence, he dropped the chalk and spun around. "Mommy."

He hurtled across the room and grasped the edge of the baby gate. Meg tried to reach over with one arm, gasped and drew up sharply. Travis's face clouded over and his bottom lip jutted forward. Ian reached over and lifted Travis over the gate, settling him into the curve of Meg's right arm.

Travis buried his face against her neck, but rolled his head sideways to peer at Ian through a tangle of dark curls. Ian tweaked his nose. "Hi, Travis."

Travis raised his hand and waved by opening and

closing his fist. Thank goodness Travis was still too young to make much of her sling. Meg called to one of the other day-care workers, "Miss Lori, can you please hand me Travis's backpack?"

"Sure, Meg." Lori grabbed the wooden train car Ian had given Travis the night before. "He was playing with this all day. I'm sure he wouldn't want to forget it."

When Lori approached the baby gate, Ian snagged the backpack from her and hung it on his arm. Travis pointed to Ian and said, "Daddy."

Meg's heart filled to bursting, but she didn't want to make a big deal out of Travis's pronouncement for his sake and Ian's. "That's right, Travis. Daddy gave that toy to you."

She glanced at Ian over Travis's head. In his otherwise impassive face, his green eyes flickered. Meg couldn't discern the emotion there, and she didn't want to. Her body and her mind suddenly felt exhausted.

Was she crazy to go through with this dinner tonight? Maybe, but she didn't want to be alone with that boarded-up window in her garage. A house full of people would ward off the heebie-jeebies. Make something about her life feel normal again, since Ian had stumbled back into it bringing murder and mayhem...and a father for Travis.

They borrowed a car seat from Eloise, and Ian secured it in the backseat all by himself. Progress. Travis fell asleep on the way home, and Ian kept his conversation to a curt minimum. Meg knew he didn't want to get into the wisdom of the dinner party tonight, and neither did she.

She no longer felt enthusiastic about it, but she didn't want to ask Ian to stay with her yet another night. He had work to do, which he'd been neglecting by running after her.

"You're going to double-check those people on yesterday's hike, aren't you? If Hans didn't kill Kayla, then somebody else on that hike did."

"Someone on the hike or someone waiting in the wings."

She tilted her head. "That's a new theory. You think maybe someone was following us or lying in wait near the lookout to the falls?"

"Maybe or maybe not." He rubbed his eyes. "I just want to find out how this is all linked to Jack."

"And I'm interfering with that."

The line of his jaw hardened. "I never said you were interfering in the case, Meg. You *are* the case now, for better or for worse."

Meg wedged her cheek against the icy window and mumbled, "For richer or for poorer, till death do us part."

"What?" His voice sharpened along with his profile.

She sighed. "Nothing."

"Do you want me to pick up anything for you? Food? Drinks? Wine? Beer?"

"There's a good Chinese place in town that delivers, and I already have enough soda and juice bags to float a boat. Don't need any alcohol. These are parents with kids. Parents don't drink and drive with the kids in the car."

"Really?" He snorted. "Because I can remember some car trips that could rival Mr. Toad's Wild Ride."

Her chest tightened and her nose tingled. "Normal parents." She brushed the back of her hand along the sleeve of his jacket. "Parents like us."

He dipped his head and glanced in the rearview

mirror, as if to make sure his son wasn't an illusion. After he pulled into her driveway and carried Travis to his bed, he settled his hands on her hips and propelled her toward the couch. "Sit down and rest. I see a teakettle on the stove. Do you want me to put some water on for tea?"

Hugging her jacket with the hole in the arm around her body, she kicked her feet up on the coffee table. "Sure, thanks."

He clanged around in the kitchen and then headed for the front door. "I'm just going to check around the property, make sure that wood over the garage window is secure."

She hunched deeper into her jacket and nodded. She gritted her teeth at the thought of being scared in her own house. She'd get her shotgun locked and loaded and take on anyone who dared cross her threshold.

Flipping her hair back, she smiled, the tough thoughts shoring up her courage. Just as the teakettle began its high-pitched whistle, Ian stomped through the front door.

"You doing okay? Everything looks fine outside." He strode into the kitchen and called out. "Tea bags?"

"They're in the cupboard next to the stove. Earl Grey would be great. Or I can get off this couch and do it myself."

Ian appeared at the kitchen entry, a steaming cup in hand. All that was missing was the apron. Meg giggled at the mental picture.

"What? You think I can't make a cup of tea?"

She sniffed the air. "It smells perfect."

He crept toward her, holding the mug in front of him. He placed it on the table with a click and snagged the phone from its cradle. "I'm leaving you with the tea and the phone, so you can call in your order. Do you need anything else?"

Meg hunched forward and wrapped her hands around the warm mug. She eyed him over the rim of the cup, through the curling steam, her eyes watering. She knew what she needed, but right now she had a dinner to throw.

She flicked her fingers toward the door. "I'm good to go. You should get back to work."

"If you need anything, call me." He stopped at the door and made a gun with his fingers, pointing in her direction. "And remember, shoot first, ask questions later."

When Ian closed the door Meg sat still, holding her breath and listening to the creaks and pings of the house. She released it with a gush and blew on her tea before sipping it. She didn't have to worry about anyone charging up to her house with a gun blazing. The guy shot at them today because they had stumbled onto the territory he was searching and guarding.

He probably tried to break in last night to look for anything belonging to Kayla. That's why he broke into Ian's hotel room. *And knocked out the maid.*

She shivered and slurped more hot tea. When she drained the last drop from the cup, she walked to the hall closet and peeked in at her rifle—stashed well within her reach for a quick grab, and well out of Travis's reach.

Then she took a bath, careful to hang her arm outside of the tub. She called in the order for the Chinese food and busied herself in the kitchen, getting paper plates and plastic utensils. She hadn't been kidding when she told Ian she'd planned a strictly casual affair.

She and the other parents at Eloise's Day Care held a rotating dinner each month, meeting at a different family's house each time. Travis was already picking up on the fact that some of his buddies had a mom and a dad. Now he did, too. How long would it last?

She spent the next hour straightening up the house and waking Travis from his nap. When the doorbell rang, her heart picked up speed. She peered through the peephole at the young man on the porch, plastic bags clutched in his hands, wound around his fingers.

She had a fleeting thought that her shooter could've taken out the delivery guy, stashed him in the bushes at the end of the driveway and picked up the cashew chicken and egg rolls.

Good thing she recognized Brendan Chu from his family's restaurant, Han Ting.

"Hi, Brendan. Is there more?"

"You ordered a lot, Ms. O'Reilly. Company tonight?" He glanced down at Travis, who had grabbed his leg. "Hey, little dude."

"Yeah, just a small party." She picked up Travis, and hitched him onto one hip and held the door wide for Brendan. "Could you put the bags on the kitchen counter?"

"What happened to your arm?" He tilted his head over the bags of food in his arms, toward the sling.

"Accident on a hike today."

He placed the bags on the counter and brushed his long bangs out of his eyes with the back of his hand. "Another accident? I heard a woman fell yesterday, and then another tourist disappeared."

"Yeah, you could say the end of the season is finishing with a bang."

"My parents aren't very happy about all this. They still need the business to tide them over until ski season."

Meg looked up at the pewter-gray sky. "Ski season

may be coming early this year. Do you need help with the rest of the bags?"

"You've got a bum arm. If my parents heard I accepted your help with the bags, they'd lock me out of the house for five days and five nights, or at least take away my cell phone." Brendan jogged down the steps and returned with the rest of the food. He accepted her tip with a big grin and scurried back to his car, as if afraid she'd change her mind and take it back.

As soon as she began to pull cartons of food from the bags, the doorbell rang again. Her gaze shot to the clock glowing on the microwave. Must be the guests arriving.

A HALF HOUR LATER, grown-ups and kids crowded Meg's small house, talking, laughing and negotiating chopsticks. She brushed off their questions about her shoulder, although talk of the two dead bodies permeated much of the conversation.

Sophia, the mom of a little girl a few months older than Travis sidled up next to Meg. "I heard Sheriff Cahill has some competition."

Meg nearly inhaled a peanut and coughed. "What are you talking about?"

Sophia pursed her lips. "Don't be coy, Meg. Word is, there's a smokin' hot FBI guy here investigating the hiker murders and doing a little recon on you, too."

Meg rolled her eyes. How did the half truths and rumors get started? But if that's what everyone believed about Ian, she didn't have any intention of correcting them. Pete must be keeping quiet about her past relationship with Ian, and Eloise must be keeping her lip zipped, too. How soon before everyone made the link between Ian Dempsey and her son, Travis Dempsey?

"Obviously, he's questioned me. I was leading the hike for both of those tourists." She poked Sophia with one of her chopsticks. "And I told you before, I'm not interested in Pete."

"Pete's interested in you. He's a fine-looking man, if wound a little tightly, and Travis really needs a dad."

"Travis has a dad." Meg spoke sharply and almost dropped her plate.

"Then maybe it's time to locate him." Sophia sauntered away and sat on the arm of her husband's chair, slanting toward him in a possessive manner.

Meg cruised the room with a trash bag dangling from her wrist. Despite the gossip about the deaths on the mountain and the ridiculous rumors about Ian, she was glad she'd gone ahead with the party. The buzz of voices, the squeals of the children and even the greasy paper plates made everything feel normal.

That feeling lasted two seconds after the last guest left.

Travis could barely keep his eyes open as Meg brushed his teeth. She tucked him into bed and he didn't even ask for a story. He did mumble one word as he burrowed into his pillow. "Daddy."

Meg peered through the slats of the blinds in Travis's room. His window looked out on the side of the house that led to the bushes where Ian had heard the intruder make his escape.

She left Travis's door open while she packed up some remaining cartons of food. She'd sent her guests home with leftovers, and they'd responded by thoroughly cleaning up after themselves.

She slid a glance toward the closet. She figured she could always sit in a rocking chair facing the front door with her rifle slung across her lap like Annie Oakley or something.

Maybe she should've just invited Ian to the party and introduced him as Travis's father…her husband. It would've quelled the rumors, and better yet, he'd still be here right now.

No. Ian had work to do. She wasn't a helpless woman like her mother; like her twin sister who'd meekly gotten into the limo with a drunk driver. They'd been so cowed by her Dad, they couldn't speak up for themselves, even when their lives depended on it.

Despite her father's disappointment, Meg remained standing. And she could take care of herself and Travis.

As she cinched up a trash bag, the doorbell rang. She froze. The doorbell rang again. She dropped the bag on the kitchen floor.

A killer wouldn't come calling at the front door.

Just in case, she tripped to the closet and dragged out the rifle. She cocked it, nice and loud, and crept toward the door. Then the banging started and she jumped back, clutching the gun to her chest.

She leaned forward and peered through the peephole. Matt. She almost collapsed on the floor in relief. What was her boss doing banging on her door in the middle of the night?

"Hold on, Matt." She leaned the rifle against the wall behind the chair and threw the dead bolt.

She yanked open the door and Matt stumbled into her house. He lurched against her and she sucked in a breath as he tugged on her injured arm. "What's wrong with you?"

His grip loosened as he slid to the floor…leaving a trail of blood on her shirt. Her mouth dropped open, but she couldn't form one word.

Chills gripped her body. Matt's voice rasped from his throat and Meg leaned over to hear his words.

"He killed me. And you're next."

Chapter Eleven

Ian's pulse quickened, and he focused the night vision binoculars on the car as it pulled up to Meg's house. A returning guest? No, he'd memorized those vehicles, and this one didn't match.

A car door flew open and a man emerged as if spit out by the vehicle. He took a few stumbling steps, not bothering to shut the door behind him. His heart thundering, Ian curled his fingers around the door handle as he sharpened the focus of his binoculars.

The pressure against his temples eased when he recognized Meg's boss Matt, staggering up the walkway. The guy looked like he'd had a few too many. Maybe that's how he relaxed, because Ian had rarely seen anyone as tightly wound as that dude.

A slice of light appeared as Meg opened the door. She must've already seen Matt through the peephole. As Ian had the binoculars trained on the two of them, Meg stumbled backward. Ian swore and launched out of the car. His hand hovered over his weapon as he charged up the walkway to the porch.

Matt lay crumpled at Meg's feet with Meg bent over him. As Ian's boots crunched the gravel, Meg's head shot up. Her mouth formed an O in her white face.

But Matt's face looked whiter.

"What the hell happened?" Ian dragged Matt from where he was bunched around Meg's feet and ankles. Matt groaned and rolled onto his back. Blood oozed from several gashes across his chest and belly.

Meg found her voice in a big way and let loose a scream that carried outside and over the mountains. A dog barked and Travis cried out from the bedroom.

"Oh no, no, no. Don't let Travis see this." She crushed her fists to her mouth.

Her body was trembling so fiercely, Ian didn't think she could walk to Travis's room. He crouched down and dragged Matt's legs into the house and shut the door behind him. He then jogged into the kitchen and grabbed a dishtowel and the phone.

Ian handed the phone to Meg. "Call 911."

He folded the dishtowel in two and applied it to Matt's fiercest wound. Travis cried out again, and Meg almost dropped the phone on Matt's head. Ian cinched Meg around the wrist and yanked her down. "Keep the pressure on. You call 911 and I'll see about Travis."

As he headed down the hall, Ian could hear Meg's shaky voice talking to the dispatcher. Outside of Travis's room, Ian took a big breath and tucked his weapon behind his back.

Ian perched on the edge of Travis's bed, where Travis was sitting up, rubbing his eyes and crying. "Hey, Travis. Did you have a bad dream?"

Travis dragged his fists down his tear-streaked face and nodded. "Dog barking."

"I hear him. Maybe he had a bad dream, too." He tugged at Travis's pajamas to get him to lie back down, but Travis fell into his lap instead.

His hand hovered above his son's head. Then he stroked one light brown curl. Travis sniffled and ran the back of his hand across his nose. Closing his eyes, he wrapped a small arm around Ian's thigh.

God, he should be doing what he could for Matt out there. He hadn't wanted to leave Meg alone with him, but she'd been in no condition to comfort Travis. He glanced down at his son and shifted his sleeping form back onto his bed.

He crept out of the room and snapped the door closed behind him. Maybe Travis would sleep through the sirens and commotion. If not, maybe his mom would be sufficiently recovered to calm his fears.

Ian strode into the living room and banged his knee against the coffee table. Meg had retrieved more towels and bunched them against Matt's chest and stomach. She was dabbing his face and mouth with a wet cloth and had hooked her arm behind his neck.

She glanced up. Her face had lost the panicked look and the wide eyes. "He's still breathing, and at least the blood's not gurgling out of him anymore."

At the first wail of the siren, Meg's shoulders rounded forward. "Thank God. How's Travis?"

"He went back to sleep." Ian kneeled beside her, placing his fingers against Matt's faint pulse. "I just hope the sirens don't wake him up again."

"I can handle him if they do. Thanks for stepping in."

He tilted a chin at Matt. "Thank *you* for stepping in."

"I wasn't going to let my boss bleed out on my living room floor."

The *whoop, whoop* of the sirens stopped and revolving blue and red lights splashed through the front window of the house. Ian eased up and opened the door to the

EMTs storming the front walkway. "I think he's been stabbed."

Ian peeled Meg's red-stained hands from Matt's body and nudged her away as the EMTs swooped in to start their hero work. She tilted her head and blew out a breath. "I think Travis is still sleeping."

The second set of sirens wailed down the street and she bit her lip. "At least he was."

Wrapping an arm around Meg's waist, Ian pulled her flush against his body. "Matt was conscious when he dragged himself up to your house. Did he say anything before he collapsed?"

"He said somebody killed him and I was next." She held her free hand in front of her, studying the blotches that resembled red wine. Her hand was as steady as the granite in the mountains beyond her front yard.

Ian tightened his hold on her, and then again, as Sheriff Cahill marched up the driveway. Cahill's eyes narrowed as his gaze darted from Matt to Ian and Meg framed in the doorway.

"I oughtta run you out of my town, Dempsey."

For the violence that seemed to follow him everywhere, or for his arm around Meg?

Pinching the bridge of his nose, Ian said, "I don't blame you, Sheriff."

Cahill loomed over Matt, the EMTs still attaching tubes and masks to him. "What happened to him, Meg?"

The EMT jabbed another needle into Matt's arm and answered Cahill without looking up. "Someone stabbed him three times."

The sheriff smacked the doorjamb. "Did it happen here during your party?"

Ian wondered how the good sheriff knew about Meg's

party, while Meg snapped, "Of course not. Matt banged on my front door and then collapsed in my arms."

"Did he say who did this?" Cahill's gaze wandered to Ian's hand resting lightly on Meg's hip.

"No."

"Did he say anything?"

Ian felt Meg's body stiffen. Then she cleared her throat, a sure indicator of a lie. "N-no."

She even had the stutter. If Cahill were any kind of cop, he'd read the signs. To his credit, the sheriff's lips tightened.

One of the EMTs sprang to his feet and jogged out to the ambulance. The other one held aloft a bottle connected to a tube that snaked into Matt's arm. "We're loading him up now. Are any of you next of kin?"

Meg visibly shuddered. "I thought you said he was going to be okay?"

"He lost a lot of blood. You'll still want to notify next of kin."

Sheriff Cahill raised his brows at Meg, as the two EMTs shifted Matt onto the gurney. "Does Matt have family in Crestville?"

"His ex-wife lives in Colorado Springs and his girl-friend is traveling for business. I'll call both of them from the hospital."

Ian sliced his hand through the air. "You're not going to the hospital. What about Travis?"

"Can you stay here with him, Ian? I want to be there for Matt. Somebody stabbed him and Matt got in his car and drove out here to…" she trailed off as a light glinted in Cahill's eyes "…to my house."

"Now, why did he do that?" Cahill started when the ambulance came to life, siren and all.

"I don't know, Pete." Meg's good arm flailed at her

side. "Maybe to warn me. Someone shoots me, someone stabs him, what next?"

"That's what I want to know." Cahill folded his arms and leaned against the doorjamb as if he had all night.

"Stay tuned." Ian shrugged. "Will Meg be safe at the hospital?"

"I'll stay with her." Cahill straightened his stance. "I want to question Matt when he regains consciousness anyway. I noticed your car isn't in the driveway, Meg. I'll give you a ride."

What *didn't* this guy know and notice about Meg?

She turned to Ian, clutching his sleeve. "Please stay with Travis. I'll be fine at the hospital, and there's nobody I'd rather leave Travis with than you."

Ian ran a hand across his mouth. How hard could it be to look after a sleeping two-year-old? "Sure, I'll stay here. But you stick close to Sheriff Cahill."

Was he crazy?

After Cahill waltzed off with Meg and bundled her in his squad car, Ian found a bucket and some rags, and scrubbed Matt's blood from the floor of Meg's entryway. What the hell had happened to Matt? Had the shooter gone after Matt in an attempt to get to Meg? But he already knew where Meg lived.

This guy was a loose cannon. The established terror organizations must be farming out their jobs to amateurs these days.

After Ian washed up, he kicked off his shoes and found the blanket he'd used the night before, folded at the foot of Meg's bed. He snagged one of her pillows, too, just because he liked the smell.

He settled on the couch, gun tucked beneath him, and shook out the blanket. Muffled cries from Travis's room had him bounding off the couch like a rock from a slingshot. He burst into the bedroom to find Travis sitting up, his blankets twisted around him.

"You awake again?" The small bed dipped beneath Ian's weight and Travis rolled toward him.

He twisted a curl around his finger. "Where's Mommy?"

"Mommy's sleeping. Is it okay if I stay with you?"

Travis studied him through large, round eyes, then blinked twice and nodded. "Daddy."

Ian swallowed the ridiculous lump that clogged his throat. "That's right, pal. Daddy's here."

MEG ENTERED THE HOSPITAL in Colorado Springs for the third time in two days—once for Travis, once for herself and now for Matt. Pete took charge and demanded information from the front desk. The unflappable clerk told him Matt's doctor would be out to talk to him soon.

Meg sank into one of the cushioned chairs in the waiting room. What had Matt meant by his statement? Why would somebody be after her? She understood the shots fired on the mountain today. She and Ian had been treading on dangerous ground. But why would this man still be after her? She didn't know anything.

Traitorously, she almost wished he'd find his damned weapon thingy and get lost. But she knew that had dangerous implications for the country, and possibly deadly implications for Jack.

She sighed and stretched. Pete dropped into the chair across from her, tipping his hat off his head. "Do you want anything from the vending machines?"

"No, thanks. I had a bunch of Chinese food tonight… about a million years ago."

"He's Travis's father, isn't he? I figured it out as soon as I heard his last name."

Tilting her head back, she closed her eyes. *Give the sheriff a gold star.* "Yes. Ian is Travis's father."

"And he ran out on him? Ran out on you?" Pete's voice sounded tight enough to make his head explode.

Without opening her eyes, Meg rocked her head back and forth on the cushion of the chair. "No, Pete. It wasn't like that. We'd already separated when I found out I was pregnant. I just didn't bother to tell him."

She heard Pete's noisy intake of air, and she opened her eyes to slits. "Who's the bad guy now?"

He sputtered. "I'm sure you had your reasons."

"Yeah, a bunch of dumb ones."

"Sheriff Cahill?" A young doctor clutching a medical chart entered the waiting room. "I'm Dr. Patel."

Pete stood up, confusion about Meg's admission still twisting the features of his face. "Good to meet you. Is Mr. Beaudry going to be okay?"

Dr. Patel glanced at the open chart as if it could give him all the answers. "He lost a lot of blood, but the EMTs did a good job stabilizing him. He's regained consciousness and he's going to make it, although he's going to have a few scars as souvenirs of this night."

Meg pressed a hand to her mouth and mumbled a prayer against her fingers.

"Can I talk to him?" Pete slid his fingers along the rim of his hat.

"Yes, but not for too long. He needs his rest." Dr. Patel gestured toward the swinging doors that led to a long hallway. "Room five-eight-three."

Meg held up her cell phone. "I called his ex-wife on the way over here. Does she need to come?"

The doctor raised his eyebrows. "Does she want to come?"

"Not really." Meg spread her hands. "I did say *ex*-wife, didn't I?"

"She doesn't need to come. Mr. Beaudry is out of danger for now. Nobody needs to make any life-or-death decisions."

"I left a message with his girlfriend, Ali, too, but she's out of town. At least she'll be able to take care of him when she returns."

Pete pointed to the chair she'd just vacated. "Wait here. I want to talk to Matt alone."

Meg thanked Dr. Patel and returned to her seat. When Pete left the room, she grabbed a magazine and flipped through it, the colors and faces on the pages as blurry as her thoughts. What *did* happen to Matt, and how did it involve her?

She started and the magazine fell from her hands as Pete blew through the door of the waiting room. His scowl didn't tell a happy story...at least for him.

"How's Matt holding up?"

Pete growled. "He looks like hell."

"D-did he tell you anything?" Meg dipped to retrieve the magazine, her hair shielding her face from Pete's probing look.

"Not much. He wants to see you."

Her heart beat double time in her chest, causing the collar of her sweater to tremble. "What did he say, Pete?"

"He said some guy in a mask came at him in the parking lot of the Rocky Mountain Adventures office in town. Matt lost his cell phone in the attack, and drove straight to your house, since everything on the main drag was closed." Pete chewed on the inside of his cheek, his dark eyes stormy and brimming with frustration.

"Well, I'm going to see him and let him know I called

Ali." Meg backed out of the waiting room. She didn't want to turn her back on Pete in his current foul mood.

She scurried down the hallway in case someone in charge changed his or her mind about visitors. When she reached room five-eight-three, she peeked into the oblong window cut into the door before pushing it open.

She tripped to a stop and the door banged her elbow— at least it didn't hit the one in the sling. Matt's pale form stretched out on white sheets about the color of his face. Tubes ran from his nose and arm and a machine beeped and hissed beside him.

He looked dead.

Meg tiptoed up to the bed and touched his cold hand. She whispered, "Matt?"

He stirred, his eyelids twitching. Maybe his conversation with Pete had worn him out. Pete had that effect on people.

"Matt?"

His hand jerked beneath hers and he clutched her wrist with a ferocious strength.

"It's Meg." She left her hand in his grasp, not wanting to get into a tug-of-war with a half-dead guy.

As his grip loosened, he rolled his head to the side and his eyelashes flickered. "Meg?"

"Yeah, it's me. The doc said you need to rest. I called Ali for you and left a message."

"Meg?" His fingers dug into her arm.

"Yeah, yeah. I'm here, Matt."

His dry lips puckered, and she dipped her head close to his mouth. His strength seemed to seep from his body and he dropped his hand. Then on a whoosh of breath, he hissed, "Run."

A river of chills cascaded down her spine and she

jerked her head back, snatching her hand from the bed. Her gaze darted toward the gray machine at his bedside, humming peacefully. Matt's breathing deepened and the creases of his face smoothed into a bland pudding.

He'd fallen asleep. The nurses must've drugged him up to relieve his pain. He'd tell her more when he could think straight. *Run?* What kind of advice was that? And why? What could these terrorists want from her or Matt? Whatever it was, it looked like Matt couldn't or didn't deliver.

She patted Matt's hand and withdrew from the room. If Pete planned to get anything out of her, he had a long night ahead of him. She pushed through the doors to the waiting room and Pete jumped up from his seat.

"Well?"

"Matt's all drugged up. He conked out while I was in there." She yawned and stretched her one arm over her head. "Can you take me home now? My shoulder's beginning to throb. I think I need a few painkillers myself."

"Sure." He clapped his hat on his head. "You must be worried about Travis."

She put her hand on Pete's arm. "No, I'm not worried about Travis, Pete. He's with his father."

Pete swallowed and a red tide washed over his face.

Good. Maybe he finally got the message. She wouldn't stand for him talking trash about Ian. If he wanted to come after her with both barrels blazing, he could have at it. *She* deserved his scorn, not Ian.

They shared a silent ride home. Meg released a long breath when her little house came into view, dark, peaceful, quiet. Ian's rental car in the driveway gave the house a secure look—probably just because it belonged to him.

Pete swung in behind it and cut the engine. "I'll walk you up to the front door. I told Dempsey I'd look after you."

She smiled at him gratefully and waited while he came around to the passenger door to help her out. Her shoulder ached now and she couldn't wait to pop a couple of pills.

She slid her key in the lock and swung open the door, avoiding the space in the entryway where Matt had collapsed. She turned toward Pete hovering in the doorway. "Thanks, Pete."

He tipped his hat and stepped off the porch. Meg locked up and dropped her purse on the table beneath the window. She tiptoed toward the couch, not wanting to wake up Ian if she could help it.

She peeked over the top of the couch and froze, a hard lump of fear forming in her belly. Ian had taken a pillow from her bed and scrunched it up on one end of the couch and had found the blanket from last night, which lay crumpled in a heap.

Pillow. Blanket. But no Ian.

She dashed for the hallway, flicking on the light and stumbling toward Travis's room. She clutched the doorjamb, swinging into the room. She stopped midswing and let out a breath.

Ian's long legs hung off the end of the toddler bed, one arm dragging off the edge to the floor. He'd curled the other arm around Travis, who was snuggled up to Ian's chest, one small hand against his father's scruffy chin.

Meg's nose tingled and tears flooded her eyes. Ian had missed so much. She'd robbed him. A tiny sob escaped her lips and she crept closer to the sleeping duo.

Ian would be sore in too many places to count if she

left him cramped in this little bed. She tugged at his dangling arm. "Ian."

He murmured and licked his lips. She squeezed his shoulder and gave him a shake. "Ian, wake up."

Ian bolted upright. Travis slid from his comfy perch, but didn't make a sound.

"What's wrong?" His hand groped beneath the bed and he slid his gun along the floor.

"Nothing." She ran her fingers along the grooves of his knuckles. "Everything's okay. I just thought you should stretch out on the couch. Was Travis crying?"

He brushed the hair from her face, cupping her jaw. His thumb roamed across her cheek, and she realized a few tears had dampened her face. He pulled her head close, meeting her forehead with his. "You've been crying."

"I-it's just seeing you here with Travis..." More hot tears crested and fell, following the path of the others.

Ian tilted up her chin and angled his mouth across hers. She welcomed his kiss, skimming her hands through his hair, inviting him closer.

He rose from the bed, bringing her with him, never breaking their connection. Reaching back, he tucked the covers around Travis. Then he swept Meg up in his solid embrace and launched out of their son's bedroom.

His kiss deepened and his tongue played with hers, as desire, hot and sweet, seeped into every muscle of her body. She felt boneless, languid and completely under Ian's spell.

When he carried her down the hallway and kicked open the door to her room, she knew he had no intention of sleeping on the couch tonight.

And she didn't mind one bit.

Chapter Twelve

Meg's lips tasted as sweet as a caramel apple at a county fair. Once he'd touched the tears on her cheeks, he couldn't find that anger that had been hitting him like punishing fists ever since he'd discovered that she'd kept Travis from him. He waited for the sucker punch to his gut again, but he could only feel the pressure of Meg's soft lips against his, which sent a wave of desire pounding through his body.

He dragged his mouth away from her sweet caress and buried it in her hibiscus-scented hair. He waited for the spear of rage to plunge into his heart. Waited for his brain to scream at him: *She kept your son from you. She didn't trust you enough to be a father.*

Nothing. No rage. Just Meg's soft gasp as he trailed his tongue along the velvety curve of her ear. She shifted in his embrace, and he realized that he still cradled her in his arms. He'd been subconsciously waiting for the hammer to come down. He didn't want to take his wife to bed. She'd cheated him out of two years of Travis's life.

Sighing, she pulled at his shirt and nuzzled his throat. Ian placed her gently on the bed. He could turn around right now, punish her for deceiving him. Punish himself.

She hooked her fingers in the waistband of his jeans, tugging him closer. "Come here. Make love to me."

Her throaty voice, thick with desire, caused his pulse to thud. He unzipped her jacket and slid it off her shoulder, her other arm still in a sling and pressed against her body. Beneath the jacket, she wore a sweater, the left sleeve snug on her injured arm.

She grabbed the sling around her neck and ducked out of it. Clutching her arm to her side, she unzipped the sweater. Ian squeezed his eyes closed in frustration as the gaping sweater revealed a T-shirt beneath.

"Believe me, if I didn't have this injured shoulder, I'd be out of these clothes in lightning speed." She tipped her chin toward him, still fully dressed. "What's your excuse?"

Could he tell her he was waiting for that anger to kick in, for the moment he could walk out on her for walking out on him? As he gazed at her beautiful, fresh face with its trace of tears, he swallowed the last of his bile.

"Ladies first." He kneeled beside her on the bed and gingerly peeled the sweater from her arm. He frowned at the T-shirt. "How'd you get this over your head in the first place?"

"Very carefully."

He grabbed the T-shirt at the neck and ripped it in two. Her eyes widened in mock horror as he wrestled the tattered shirt over her bandaged shoulder. "I'll replace it."

"It was vintage." With one hand, she fumbled with the buttons on his shirt. "I'm at a distinct disadvantage here."

He finished the job on the buttons, shrugged out of his shirt and yanked his T-shirt over his head. "Don't worry. I've been undressing myself for years."

"And you do a really good job." She splayed her hands across his chest, and he sucked in a breath as she lightly dug her nails into his flesh.

With one hand he reached back and released her bra. "I'm just generally good at taking clothes off…mine and others'."

"I can see that." She picked up her tattered T-shirt with two fingers and dropped it over the edge of the bed.

Ian leaned forward, gathering her breasts in his hands. His thumbs traced their round smoothness until he pinched her nipples between thumb and forefinger. A soft moan brushed his forehead as Meg's head fell back.

He kissed the inviting hollow of her throat and then formed a dotted line down her chest with the tip of his tongue. He raked the stubble of his beard over her soft skin and she bounced up from the mattress. He captured one breast in his hand and toyed with her nipple, trailing his smooth lips across it first, followed by his rough beard.

Inarticulate sounds formed in the back of her throat, but she seemed incapable of any other kind of response except to offer herself up to him like a delectable feast. She leaned back on one hand, and he cupped her other breast, switching his attention to this peaked nipple, rosy with want.

When he had her panting, he stopped his play and suckled her nipple into his mouth. She gasped and threaded her hand through his hair to push his face against her swollen breast.

His erection strained against his jeans, and he rolled to the side, placing her hand on his crotch. She struggled to sit up, brushing her breasts against his bare arm. He shivered and then gulped as she traced the outline of his hard desire.

"Mmm, I thought you left your gun under the bed."

"Wouldn't do me much good under there now, would it?"

She tugged at his zipper. "Help me out here, unless you plan to shoot those bullets into your boxers."

He laughed and rolled off the mattress, opening his fly on the way. He yanked off his jeans and boxers in one smooth move and rejoined her on the bed, pulling the covers from the bed.

Meg crawled onto the sheets and pointed to her own jeans. "I think I'm going to need help taking off my clothes until my shoulder heals."

"I'll volunteer for that job." He raised his hand. Then he unzipped her fly, slid his hands down her bare skin and inched her jeans off her body. By the time the jeans lay in a circle around her ankles, he'd run his hands down her hips, thighs and calves and had her quivering against the sheets.

Her lashes fluttered. "Would that kind of service be included in all the undressing?"

"Absolutely." He yanked the pants from her feet and tossed them over his shoulder. Straddling her hips, he skimmed his erection along her belly.

Her eyes flew open and she grabbed him...hard...just the way he liked it. And she knew it. Her grip tightened and she pumped him, as he growled, rocking forward, trying to remember his grudge against her. Her thumb circled his head, and he gritted his teeth.

He knew the way she liked it, too.

Pulling away from her grip, he nudged her legs open with his knee. He settled one hand on each of her inner thighs, spreading them apart, his calluses rasping against her silky skin. She curled her good arm beneath her head to watch him. She liked that part, too.

Locking his gaze onto her smoky blue eyes, he kissed her navel and her abdomen, softer now after the birth of Travis. He licked one hip bone and nibbled the other. He trailed lower, alternating between licks, bites and kisses. A different sound for each assault puffed from her lips.

Then he slid the tip of his tongue down lower still and she moaned, a deep, dark sound of need. Her musky, sweet flavor filled his mouth and he drank deeply. He teased her with his tongue and suckled with his lips until her head thrashed on the pillow and she whimpered, breathless and on the edge. His for the taking.

After burrowing into her creamy wetness with his mouth, he pulled back. She cried out and dug her heels into his buttocks, riding him, urging him onward. He blew gently on her heated flesh. She gasped. One flick of his tongue. Two flicks. She pulsed and throbbed beneath his exquisite torture.

Three flicks. Back and forth and back. Her hips rose slowly and his mouth followed, never leaving his own private banquet. She squirmed beneath him, but he dug his fingers into her rounded hips.

Once athletic and angular, Meg's body now curved in all the right places. Pregnancy and motherhood had smoothed all her sharp edges. Her new femininity drove him mad with passion. His erection ached heavy and hard between his legs. But he had a job to finish. And he never left a job undone.

Four flicks. Back and forth and back and forth. The final flick did the trick. Her pelvis bucked once, and then she exploded. She rocked against him in a rhythmic motion, seeking contact. He slid two fingers inside her wet passage and she closed around him. Then he moved up her body and kissed her slack mouth as she melted beneath him.

He kissed her bandage. "Okay?"

She wrapped her legs around his hips in answer. He didn't need to use his hand to guide himself inside her honeyed walls. He knew the way by heart. He slid inside, the coil in his belly tightening as he felt her heat swallow him inch by inch.

They moved together, their bodies singing the same melody—no, not the same. His body sang the melody and hers complemented it with a sweet harmony, completing the song, completing him.

He rose on his elbows to stare into her face, the face he'd memorized and never forgotten, not for one second. He drove harder and she matched him, raising her hips to meet him, their bodies sealing against each other again and again. Only to come apart.

His climax came hard, hot and long. He wanted to spill into her, plant his seed, make another baby. One she couldn't keep from him.

SMILING, MEG TRAILED a hand between her breasts, the sweat slick on her cooling skin. Ian appeared in the doorway, filling it with his impressive frame…impressive, naked frame.

She extended her arm and wiggled her fingers. "Come here."

"Do you want your water?" He held out a glass as he crossed into the room.

"I want you."

"You just had me, lock, stock and barrel."

"I remember the lock and even the stock, but I'm not

sure about the barrel." A tingle rushed down her legs, curling her toes. "Can I have the barrel, too?"

He sat on the edge of the bed, placing the glass next to the lamp that cast a soft glow over his forearm, corded with tight, tense muscle. "How's your shoulder?"

"I forgot all about it." She crinkled her forehead, wondering why Ian hadn't jumped back into bed with her. She patted the place beside her and then smoothed the bedspread, suddenly unsure of herself. "A-are you coming back to bed?"

He dipped down and pulled on his boxers. "It's late, Meg. Or rather, it's early in the morning. Won't Travis be waking up soon?"

"Probably." She pulled the covers up to her chin.

"I know I've been a father for just a few days, but I don't think it's a good idea for Travis to find me in your bed. It's too fast."

Ouch. Meg fisted her hands in the sheets. He'd taken a shot and hit the bull's eye. "Well, your parental instincts are good, and your blanket is still on the couch."

He scooped up his clothes. "How's Matt doing? Did he regain consciousness?"

"Enough to give Pete absolutely no information." She gulped her water to wash down the lump in her throat.

"And how about you? Did he give you any information?"

She licked her lips, washing away the last traces of Ian's kisses. "He told me to run, then he conked out."

Ian stopped at the door and whipped around, hugging his clothes to his chest. "What? He told you to run?"

At least she'd spiked his interest in her again. Is that all it took? A little danger? She snuggled back against her pillow. "I think he was delirious."

"Why would the terrorists come after Matt, and why would Matt think you were in danger?"

"I don't know." Meg stifled a yawn. Fear had been her constant companion these past two days, and now fatigue wanted in on the party. "I need some sleep. It's going to be a long day at work tomorrow, with Matt in the hospital."

"It's going to be a long day at work for me tomorrow, too. I'm going back to that spot in the gorge."

That woke her up like a slap in the face. "You are?"

"The case has to be there. Why else would our friend be guarding that area like a mama grizzly with her cub?"

"But he must not know where it is, or else he'd grab it and go. What's he waiting for? Why is he stabbing local tour guides and strangling tourists?"

"I don't know, but I'm going to find out." He slipped through the door and paused on the threshold. "Good night, Meg. It was…I was…" He closed the door.

Meg slumped against the pillows. It was…he was… totally amazing. What just happened? She bit her lip and turned out the light. She punched her pillow. She knew.

No matter how torrid the kisses, no matter how urgent the touches, no matter how hot the sex, Ian couldn't forgive her for Travis.

MEG WOKE UP with her arms wrapped around her pillow. She tossed the poor, lumpy substitute for Ian across the floor and rolled to an upright position.

She fingered the bandage on her shoulder. Felt like she'd banged it into a wall, nothing like what she'd imagined a gunshot wound would feel like. But then the bullet had only grazed her, skimming off a little bit of her flesh.

Heck, she'd had worse injuries banging against the side of a sheer rock face.

Stretching the arm in front of her, she wiggled her fingers and bent her elbow—all parts in working order. Her nostrils twitched at the smell of waffles and coffee. She struggled out of the tangled covers and snagged her robe from a hook on the back of the bedroom door.

She peeked into Travis's room on her way to the kitchen. She doubted her two-year-old son would've been traumatized by finding a man in his Mom's bed, but maybe father did know best. It would've been a first for Travis, since Meg hadn't had a man in her bed, or anywhere else, since her separation from Ian.

"You found the waffles." She wedged a shoulder against the fridge and watched Ian navigate the coffeemaker.

"Hope you don't mind." He forked one and dropped it onto an empty plate. "You mentioned yesterday you had some more frozen, so I rummaged around your freezer. I pulled out a couple for you and Travis, too."

She pressed her lips together. He'd rummaged around her body last night, why would she care about an appliance? "No problem, and thanks for thinking of us."

Thanks for thinking of us? She sounded like one of those twits from her sister's debutante balls.

He turned with a plate in his hand. "Take this one. I'll put another in the microwave for myself. How's your shoulder?"

"It feels bruised mostly." She took the plate from him and squeezed a dribble of syrup on the waffle. "It's really not that bad."

"But you're not leading any hikes."

Meg opened her mouth, ready to argue with him just because his statement sounded so much like a command.

She closed it around a bite of sticky waffle and shook her head. "With Matt down and out and me not one hundred percent, I have a feeling we're going to be canceling a lot of hikes."

"Good, because I'm going to be out there on my own today."

She swallowed. "You really think the device is in that gorge?"

"I'm positive. Your shooter wouldn't be protecting it otherwise."

"What do you think is in the case, Ian?" She drew patterns in the syrup with the tines of her fork. He'd always shut her down in the past when she'd asked questions about his work. She didn't dare look at him now. "Could it be a danger to Crestline?"

"I don't think so." Drawing his brows together, he spread butter on his waffle and then sliced it in two. "Our sources indicate it's a device, not a full-fledged weapon, but something very necessary to complete the arming of a weapon."

"Ugh. The sooner you get it out of here, the better." At least Ian was opening up more, even if he had shut her down earlier this morning. "I'm going to check in on Matt and then help out at the office. Do you need any supplies?"

"No, but if Matt can give you anything more than a warning to run, let me know. A description of this guy would be good. He's like a phantom."

"Are you going to have a cell phone or radio out there? The cell reception is bad to nonexistent. You really should take a radio in case you run into any trouble."

"I'll take you up on that offer. How about I drive you to the office and I can pick up a radio there before I head out?"

"That works for me, especially since I still don't have my car."

"Do you think you can drive now?"

Meg rotated her shoulder, wincing only a little. "I can drive."

"We drop Travis off at Eloise's first, right?"

He knew Travis's schedule already. "Yeah. I'm going to get ready to go."

FORTY-FIVE MINUTES LATER, Meg scooped up a fed-and-polished Travis and kissed the top of his head. "Daddy's going to give us a ride today."

Travis pointed to Ian pulling on his jacket. "Daddy sleep wit me."

"I know." She ruffled his hair. "Was he as warm and snuggly as Mommy?"

"Hey, that's an unfair leading question. Nobody's as warm and snuggly as Mommy." Ian zipped up his jacket and winked.

Meg took a deep breath and swung open the front door. The man would give her whiplash with his changing moods. He wanted her. He pushed her away. Which was it? Could he forgive her or not?

Maybe she'd better back off and give him space, even when it seemed as if he didn't want it. He didn't know what he wanted right now, except Travis. She knew he wanted Travis.

And the thought scared her.

What if he wanted Travis but didn't want her as part of the bargain? She'd have to share Travis with him. She hugged Travis tighter until he squirmed in her grasp.

She didn't want to share.

An hour later, Meg banged the phone down at the

front desk of Rocky Mountain Adventures. "They won't tell me anything."

Scott perched on the edge of the desk. "The hospital?"

"I'm not next of kin." She put her head in her hands. "Do you think that means Matt is worse?"

"Not necessarily. When's Ali getting back into town? Is the hospital going to let her see him?"

"He may have her listed as his emergency contact or something. Matt asked to see me last night when he was barely conscious. You'd think they'd take that into consideration."

"Why don't you just call Pete? He probably has the inside scoop."

"I hate asking Pete for favors."

"You hate asking anyone for favors, Meg. You're allergic to it."

She chewed on her lip. Sometimes she let that particular allergy cloud her common sense. She picked up the phone and dialed Pete's private cell phone number.

"Sheriff Cahill."

"Pete, it's Meg. How's Matt doing this morning? The hospital won't tell me anything."

He paused and her heart thumped so loudly, surely Pete could hear it over the phone. "What is it?"

"Sorry to tell you this, Meg, but Matt hasn't regained consciousness since your visit last night."

Meg slumped back in the chair. "Oh my God. Is he in danger? I thought the doc said he was in the clear."

"Doctors don't know anything."

Meg forgave Pete his bitterness, since his mom had passed away from cancer six months ago and he'd been on a roller-coaster ride with her doctors.

"So you think it's serious?"

"Someone stabbed him three times in the gut. Of course it's serious. I hope Dempsey finds what he's looking for and gets the hell out of Crestline."

Meg checked her watch and blew out a breath. "You may get your wish today, Pete."

But Pete's hopes happened to collide with her dreams. She didn't want Ian the hell out of Crestline. She didn't want that at all.

Chapter Thirteen

Ian straddled the log and reached for his water bottle stuffed in the side of his backpack. He'd hiked to yesterday's crime scene, the slick, yellow police tape now flapping in the crisp wind. A little farther and he'd get to the scene of the second crime, where the desperate terrorist had nicked Meg.

Of all the places to dump their cargo, these guys had to pick Meg's mountain. What kind of lousy coincidence was that?

Or was it?

Ian took another gulp of water. When Riley, his Navy SEAL buddy from Prospero, had uncovered the link between the Velasquez drug cartel and a terrorist group out of Afghanistan, Prospero's old nemesis, Farouk, had his dirty hands all over the deal. Riley had to let Farouk escape with the money from the drug deal, and Farouk had used it to purchase a weapon from Slovenka…the weapon dumped out of that airplane. But why had he scuttled the package over these mountains?

When Farouk's terrorist cell had been battling Prospero in the Middle East, Farouk had made it his personal mission to find out as much information as he could about the Prospero team members. Ian had always believed in Farouk's complicity in the death of Riley's wife, although Ian had never divulged his suspicions to Riley.

How much did Farouk know about Ian's marriage to Meg? How much did he know about Meg? Ian snapped a piece of bark from the tree trunk and chucked it into the thin air. Maybe Farouk had planned to drop the suitcase here all along, even before Buzz forced the plane down.

Ian pushed up from the log and clapped his gloved hands together. Right now he had to find that elusive suitcase before Farouk's guy found it. And it had to be somewhere in this area.

He raised his binoculars and tracked across the dense foliage clinging to the side of the mountain. The plant life grew more sparsely where the falls cut through the mountainside, spilling sparkling water over tumbled boulders. Several ledges jutted out from the solid granite, resembling huge steps for a giant to climb to the top of the mountain.

Ian zeroed-in on one of the outcroppings, his pulse picking up speed. While most of the slabs cut into the mountainside were bereft of foliage, one stood out for the greenery that clustered around it. Prospero had trained him to look for the oddity, for the out-of-place.

Ian studied the cliff with his naked eye. To reach it, a human being would have to scale the side of the mountain with rock climbing gear, or at least be an expert free-style rock climber. There was no way someone climbed up there and dragged branches and leaves along with him. He huffed out a cold breath and shook his head.

Two hours later, after trudging in a big circle, Ian headed back toward the crime scene and picked his way up the makeshift trail he and Meg had forged the day before. He had to make a decision about Meg and stick with it. Running hot and cold wasn't doing either of them any favors. He wanted to punish her for keeping Travis a secret, but he'd be punishing himself, too...and Travis.

Truth is, having Meg in his arms last night felt like coming home. He hadn't put aside his anger so much as other, more pressing, emotions had shoved it out of the way. The fact that he understood her reasons for keeping Travis away from him cut the deepest. Even though he knew on one level she had her own demons to slay, his just kept popping up their ugly heads.

He reached the cusp of the ridge and hauled himself over. He shoved to his feet, brushing twigs and leaves from his jeans.

"See anything?"

Ian jerked his head up and raised his brows at Meg, hiking boots planted on the trail in front of him. He cursed under his breath and reached for his water. That could've been anyone standing on the trail, catching him with his pants down. He'd had too many distractions on this job.

"Not much, but I did notice something unusual about the outcroppings around the falls. What are you doing here, anyway?" He wiped his mouth with the back of his hand.

Meg shoved her hands in her pockets and hunched her shoulders. "Lunch break."

"How's the shoulder?"

"I took off the sling, didn't need it." She held out her arm and wiggled her gloved fingers. "It's just sore, and a couple of ibuprofen takes care of that."

"You were lucky."

"You were lucky, too. I think he meant to shoot you, and I just happened to stumble in the way."

He'd thought that, too, until Matt staggered onto Meg's doorstep and collapsed. "How's Matt doing?"

Meg closed her eyes and pulled the collar of her jacket up to her chin. "He lost consciousness after talking to me last night, and hasn't regained it since."

Ian whistled through his teeth. "That's not good. And Cahill still has no description of the man who attacked him and why."

"No description and no motive, but I think we all know the attack is linked to your investigation. What could someone looking for that case possibly gain by killing Matt?"

"Unless they think he saw something, too." Ian narrowed his eyes and shifted slightly toward the gorge.

"What about those outcroppings?" Meg pointed toward the waterfall. "You said you noticed something unusual."

"Almost all of them are bare." He slipped the binoculars over his head and handed them to Meg, even though this angle didn't afford them a good look at those ledges to the left of the falls. "Except one."

Tilting her head, she took the binoculars from him and peered through them. "I know what area you mean. What's wrong with the one ledge?"

"Nothing wrong with it, but it looks different. It has clumps of greenery on it that look like branches. Can trees grow there?"

She shrugged, thrusting the binoculars out toward him. "It's nature. Anything's possible, but I can't see anything from here."

"Is there any way to get up there short of rock climbing?" Meg had said she knew this mountain better than anyone…except maybe Matt.

"To get on the actual ledges?" She wrinkled her nose.

"No. That cliff face is a rock climber's paradise, and we have bolts on the way up to prove it. You can look down on those outcroppings from a trail up top, but you can't get down, unless you want to jump, and you'd have to be incredibly precise to hover a helicopter near the falls."

A thrill of excitement raced up Ian's spine. "How long is that hike from here?"

"It's a good two hours." Her eyes widened. "Are you thinking of going up there?"

He grabbed her good shoulder and spun her around. "Look at the location, Meg." He pointed toward the falls in the distance. "Kayla could've had a clear view from the observation deck." Then he gestured toward the gorge beneath them. "And there's even a better perspective from down there."

She nodded slowly, a light sparking her blue eyes. "You think the suitcase might be up there?"

"It's a possibility, the first good lead we've had since this whole thing started." He glanced at his watch. "Do we still have time to get up there?"

She twisted her wrist and peeked beneath the sleeve of her jacket. "It's just past noon. We have plenty of time."

"Then let's go." He tilted his chin in a challenge. Meg never could resist a challenge.

She grinned, the cold air whipping color into her cheeks. "All right, then. We've already canceled a few hikes today, so we should have this side of the mountain to ourselves."

"And in case we don't..." Ian peeled open his jacket to reveal his weapon tucked into its holster.

"Good thinking." Meg glanced over her shoulder, a whisper of fear huffing against the back of her neck. This might be a great opportunity to reconnect with Ian, hiking together like old times, but she'd better not forget their goal...or the forces against them.

Once she'd grown bored with the office work this morning, her eyes kept straying toward the window. Knowing Ian was out there challenged her attention span even more, until she shut down her computer and raced out to join him. She'd told herself she needed to be out there for Matt and for Kayla, but she'd told herself so many little white lies over the past two years, she recognized one when it snuck up and whispered in her ear.

"Lead the way." Ian nudged her back. "Are you sure that shoulder's okay?"

"It's a dull ache, pretty disappointing for a gunshot wound."

"Count yourself lucky. We don't want him to get it right next time."

Swallowing hard, Meg charged up the trail before she changed her mind. During their marriage, she'd always wanted Ian to share his work with her. This time around, he'd made all her dreams come true tenfold. Would she live to regret it?

FOR ALMOST TWO HOURS, they made good time up the sloping trail that zigzagged up the side of the mountain. They stopped occasionally for a water break or to munch on a snack. Meg reveled in sharing the outdoors with Ian again, and he deferred to her knowledge of the terrain.

He understood, after her upbringing in her father's house, that she needed to feel useful, wanted others to take her seriously. But maybe she'd outgrown that desire, or maybe Travis fulfilled it, because she didn't bristle every time Ian held the bushes back for her or cupped her elbow over a particularly rough spot.

He helped her and she helped him, sharing like adults. He'd be that kind of father, too.

"The source of the falls is right around that ridge, isn't it?" Ian waved his hand where the trail took a sharp left turn.

Nodding, she brushed the hair from her forehead with the back of her hand. "Not much farther. And we should have a clear view of that ledge that caught your attention from below."

A brisk breeze rattled the branches of the trees, which showered leaves on the path before them. Meg crunched along the trail, her heart pounding more from excitement than from exertion. If they found the suitcase, this adventure could end here and now.

Then what?

Ian scrambled across the boulders ahead of her and then turned and held out his hand. She gave it to him without rancor, without fear that it made her less for accepting help.

He pulled her next to him and plucked a leaf from her hair. "Are you ready for this, Meg-o?"

She blew out a frosty breath. "I'm ready."

They both inched toward the edge of the cliff, slippery with water from the stream that fed the waterfall. Ian dropped to his knees and slithered on his belly toward the drop-off. "Damn!"

"What is it?" Meg crouched beside him. She flattened her body and lay shoulder-to-shoulder with Ian.

He pointed, his finger drawing circles in the air. "That's the ledge. It's covered with branches and debris."

"That's good." She sucked in a breath.

"Good? How's that good?"

"Look above you." Meg tilted her head back, gesturing at the sky with one arm. "No trees overhanging."

Ian twisted his head to the side. "You're right."

"You know what that means?"

She felt the muscles in his body coil through his jacket, his frame tense and ready. "That pile of foliage down there didn't get there on its own," he said.

"Which means," she continued, the words tumbling from her lips, "someone put it there."

"To hide something."

"To hide a suitcase."

Ian rose to his haunches, testing the edge of the cliff with the toe of his boot. "Is there a way down from here?"

Meg snorted. "Not if you value your life." She rolled onto her back and scooted into a sitting position. "I guess our friend values his life, too. That's why he did a cover-up instead of a rescue."

"So he knows where it is." Ian scratched his jaw. "He just can't get to it."

"But we can." Meg grabbed Ian's forearm, adrenaline zinging through her veins. "Our guy can't rock climb. He'd need a permit for this mountain, and he doesn't want to expose himself. And he can't get a chopper up here, or at least he can't find anyone crazy enough to make the attempt. He must have some other plan, or he's waiting for reinforcements."

Ian rested his forearms on his knees. "Maybe that's why he went after Matt."

"Matt?" Meg blinked.

"Can Matt intercede and get someone a rock climbing permit, or do the climb himself?"

The blood rushed to Meg's head and she closed her eyes against the dizziness. "Of course."

"Maybe this guy asked Matt and Matt refused."

"Why would Matt refuse?" Meg pressed her fingers against her temples. The thrill of the adventure had obscured the danger...for just a minute, until Ian mentioned Matt. "We get climbers occasionally. He wouldn't have thought the request out of line."

"Unless the manner of the request struck him as odd. Maybe Matt sensed something hinky and refused the request. Maybe the guy came on too strong and offered money—a payoff to keep things hush-hush."

"We can't ask him now."

"Matt warned you, told you to run, right?" Ian reached out and squeezed her knee. Her face must be reflecting her horror at the turn of the conversation.

"Do you think this man, this terrorist, had me pegged as the next one on his list to ask?"

"It makes sense."

"But he didn't. Nobody has approached me about a permit to climb or about making a climb myself."

"Things must've gone downhill quickly during his conversation with Matt. Obviously, the guy's not going to waltz in after that and start asking questions."

"So what's he going to do now? Just wander around down in the gorge and shoot at anyone who comes close to a vantage point for this ledge?"

"You said it." Ian pushed to his feet, extending his hand. "Maybe he's waiting for reinforcements."

Meg shivered and brushed a drop of rain from her cheek. "We'd better get back down. We don't want to get caught in the snow, even a light dusting."

Ian jerked his thumb over his shoulder. "Tomorrow I climb."

"Tomorrow *we* climb."

"Don't be stubborn, Meg." He grabbed her around the

waist and pulled her snug against his side. "Your shoulder's still hurting. You're not going rock climbing."

She wriggled in his grasp, but he held her tight. "But I've done it before. I can guide you up, Ian. We can lead climb, which will be so much safer than free climbing. I want to help you."

"And I want your help, Meg-o, but not with a bum shoulder. It's too dangerous." He rested his chin on top of her head and she slumped against his chest.

Ian's reasons for telling her *no* had nothing to do with her father's reasons. Ian had her safety in mind and her father had his ego. Had she finally learned to recognize the difference?

Ian rubbed his beard across her hair, catching strands with each pass. "Besides, I'm going to need someone riding shotgun. I'm going to be exposed on the side of that cliff, a sitting duck. You need to have my back, Meg." He pulled away and wedged a gloved finger beneath her chin. "Do you have my back, Meg?"

Her chest rose and fell. "I do now, Ian."

He dipped his head, slanting his mouth across hers. His lips felt warm and inviting and she took the plunge, closing her eyes and opening her mouth to his probing tongue.

How had she survived three long years without her husband?

She knew now, she never wanted to be separated from him again. Could he forgive her for Travis? Could she convince him that her reasons never included doubts about his ability to be a good father?

He plowed his fingers through her hair, the strands sticking to the suede trim on his gloves. He whispered against her aching lips, "God, I missed you."

Her mouth parted, sucking his words into her soul.

Then his lips brushed her cheek. "Your face is cold, Meg. Let's hike back and plan our assault for tomorrow."

She'd rather plan her assault on him tonight. She dropped her hands from his back, where she'd been about to slip them lower. The man still acted like a drug on her senses. His kiss caused her to lose all concept of place, time and…danger.

Did she have the same effect on him? If so, he'd had another good reason for not mixing business and pleasure—it could be hazardous to his health. Her own issues with her father had blinded her to all of Ian's good and noble intentions.

She stuffed her hands in her pockets. "Let's go. I'll file a permit for you when we get back, and get you outfitted."

By the time they returned to the Rocky Mountain Adventures office, silence greeted them. A note on the door indicated that all hikes had been suspended for the week.

Meg worried her lower lip. "I hope there's not more bad news about Matt."

She slipped her key in the door and nudged it with her hip. She shuffled through the papers on the desk while she cradled the telephone receiver between her jaw and shoulder and punched the message button.

Ian raised his brows. "Anything?"

Meg held her finger to her lips and listened to a couple of messages from disgruntled tourists with hiking plans. Plopping the phone on the desk, she shook her head. "Nothing about Matt."

"Would Sheriff Cahill know? Do you want to give him a call?" Ian scooped up the phone and held it out to her.

Meg took the phone from him, balancing it in her

palm, as if weighing its heft. "Should we call in the sheriff's department to help out tomorrow? Maybe some of the deputies could stand guard while you climb?"

"No." Ian snatched the phone from her hand. "I can't allow that, Meg. What part of 'covert operation' don't you understand? If the sheriff's department shows up, then the press shows up and this thing gets played out on the national stage. That would have dire consequences for the mission. If the CIA or the FBI gets its hands on this weapon, Prospero will lose any chance of discovering more information to help Jack. The CIA doesn't care about him. The Agency has already written him off as a traitor. Hell, maybe the Agency had a hand in setting him up."

"You guys are really paranoid, aren't you?" She held out her hand, snapping her fingers. "Okay. I'll follow your lead. I won't tell Pete anything. Heck, he already suspects we're holding out on him."

"Haven't you been holding out on Pete all along? What's once more?" Ian winked.

A hot blush marched across her cheeks. "You make it sound like I'm a tease. I never led Pete on. He knew I was still married."

Ian held out the phone, his eyes never leaving hers. "And don't you forget it."

She got Pete on the first try. Covering the mouthpiece with her hand, she whispered to Ian, "Matt's still unconscious."

Meg ended the call and tapped the receiver against her hand. "So Matt hasn't regained consciousness and Pete hasn't discovered anything nefarious about Hans Birnbacher, except that he overstayed his ninety-day welcome in the States."

"So he came in as a tourist and stuck around. Of

course, the real Hans Birnbacher may not even know he's dead. Identities can be stolen and appropriated. Happens all the time."

The hair on the back of Meg's neck quivered. Maybe Ian had been right during their years together—the less she knew about his business the better.

She flicked her watch. "Time to pick up Travis, just as soon as I file your rock climbing permit, which I can expedite. Y-you're coming over tonight, right? I mean to work out our plan for tomorrow."

"Of course. I'm not leaving you two alone tonight. You pick up Travis and I'll go back to my hotel to shower and change." He pointed to the back of the office. "Can I check out the rock climbing gear while you work on that permit?"

Meg powered on the computer and then tossed her keys to Ian. "All the stuff is locked up in the back. Help yourself."

By the time she hit the key to send off Ian's rock climbing permit, he'd returned to the front of the office loaded down with ropes, carabiners, a harness and a variety of draws, slings and grips.

"Looks like you're leading an expedition to Everest, instead of doing a solo climb."

The equipment clanked and creaked as he strode past her toward the door. "This expedition is more dangerous than Everest."

Meg sucked in a breath and held it as she powered down the computer. Would the danger of this mission make Ian rethink his decision to allow her to help him tomorrow? Did she want him to?

After all, what did she have to prove anymore? She'd already lost a mother, a twin sister, a marriage. Did she really want to lose her life to assert her independence?

IAN LOADED THE TRUNK of his rental car with the gear he probably wouldn't need and collapsed in the driver's seat. Exhaustion seeped into his bones. If he had to keep walking this tightrope with Meg, his muscles would clench up and lock.

He didn't want her anywhere near this mountain when he climbed that cliff face tomorrow. If he had to hog-tie her and stash her in his trunk to keep her away, he'd do it. Motherhood may have softened her body, but it hadn't done anything to wear down those prickles that sprang up whenever someone tried to tell her what to do. She couldn't stop equating every challenge with her father's attempt to dominate her life.

Had he done any better in slaying his personal demons? He enjoyed being around Travis, but the kid scared the hell out of him.

He waved at Meg in the rearview mirror as she locked up the office and climbed into her SUV. As he followed her down the road into Crestville, he punched in Buzz Richardson's number on his cell.

"Hey, Ian. What's up? You find that weapon yet?"

"I might have. That's why I'm calling. I need your help. Where are you?"

"I'm in D.C. There's been chatter about President Okeke's visit to the UN and Slovenka's name has come up a few times."

Ian's nostrils flared. Okeke had been elected president of a newly formed African nation. The U.S. was keeping its eye on him for his former ties to terrorists, but he'd been elected in a seemingly democratic process. The Americans had decided to play hands-off...for now.

"What kind of chatter?"

"Assassination attempt."

Ian cursed into the phone. "And because Slovenka's

name has been mentioned in connection to this plot, the colonel thinks it's linked to Jack's disappearance."

"It's like pieces of a puzzle. We start with the bits on the edge and work our way inside. That's why Colonel Scripps sent me out here, and…ah…Raven's been assigned as Okeke's translator."

"What's the colonel trying to do? Isn't one assassination attempt enough?" Ian beeped his horn and waved as he pulled into the parking lot of his hotel, and Meg continued toward Travis's day care.

"Raven and I split on okay terms. Speaking of splits, I'm sure you've run into Meg in Crestville. How's that going for you?"

Ian pulled into a parking space, killed the engine and rubbed the back of his neck. "That's why I called."

Closing his eyes, Ian told Buzz about Meg's involvement and her expectations for tomorrow. "I can't allow her to be anywhere near that ledge when I make my climb."

Buzz whistled. "No kidding."

"That's why I need your help. You need to take a red-eye or fly your own plane. Just get yourself out here so you can watch my back while I scale that cliff face and retrieve the suitcase. And I need to do it before Slovenka's customer sends for reinforcements."

"I can get out there tomorrow, but probably not until later in the afternoon. Will that work?"

"It's going to have to." Ian thanked his friend and rolled into his hotel room for a shower and a change of clothing.

When he got out of the shower, he rubbed a circle in the steam on the mirror. He ran a hand through his damp hair and hunched forward on the vanity. One way or another, he had to convince Meg to stay home.

He tried on his best seductive smile for his reflection, and blew out a breath, creating more fog on the mirror. He'd better get ready to sweet talk his wife—either that or tie her to the bedpost…or maybe he'd do both.

MEG PULLED UP to the curb in front of Eloise's Victorian house. Eloise's Day Care had been a Godsend for the working parents of Crestville. Large enough so that the kids got some variety in both other kids and day-care teachers, but small enough to lend the right air of intimacy and coziness for the kids.

Meg knocked, using the brass knocker, and Eloise herself answered the door. "A little late, aren't you Meg?"

With her brow furrowed, Meg checked her watch. "Not too late, am I?" Eloise charged extra for each minute a parent picked up late.

"Not too late, but you're usually here earlier, and Travis has been antsy." Eloise waved her into the living room, which she kept off-limits to the kids.

Meg pressed against the baby gate that separated the toddler play area from Eloise's living room, and waved to Travis, who was punching his fist into a lump of clay. She grinned. She wanted her son to work out all his aggressions before he came home. She didn't want to scare off Ian with a two-year-old tantrum.

"Get your backpack from the hook, Travis. Time to come home." Only one other toddler occupied the play area, and guilt rolled through Meg like a tumbleweed leaving prickly burrs in its wake. "Oh, I really am late, if Sierra's the only toddler left."

Eloise handed Meg a bag with Travis's empty lunch containers. "It looks like we may have another toddler joining us. A couple from Colorado Springs dropped by today for a tour, and they're supposed to return tomorrow to pick up the paperwork. A very affectionate couple, looked more like they were on a honeymoon than shopping for day care."

"The more the merrier, and the more loving the better, I suppose." Meg scooped up Travis in her arms and said goodbye to Eloise. She chattered to him in the car about dinner and Daddy and new friends. By the time she reached home, Travis had conked out. She carried him inside and tucked him into bed for a nap, and then pulled out all the ingredients for chicken enchiladas. Ian liked his food spicy…and his sex spicier.

Could she win him over with sex? Did she really want to? She knew he had some kind of battle royale going on between his desire for her and his resentment toward her for keeping him away from Travis.

The lust seemed to be winning out over anger. Most of the time.

She rotated her shoulder and eased out a breath. She barely noticed the pain now, and she'd removed the bandage and sling, replacing them both with a simple gauze pad. Her wound resembled a rectangle with raised edges on the side. Not serious at all.

Certainly not serious enough to keep her from climbing tomorrow, if Ian needed her.

SHE ROLLED THE FINAL corn tortilla around the chicken filling and nestled it in the pan beside the other enchiladas. Then she ladled spicy red sauce over the rows of neatly wrapped tortillas and sprinkled cheese over everything.

Ian's lips would be hot tonight. Her own lips quirked into a grin as she shoved the pan in the oven. Guess she'd decided to take the low road and overwhelm him with hot sex so he'd forget all about his hot anger.

She ducked into the shower and then pulled on a pair of black leggings and a long blue sweater. Ian knocked on the door as she put the finishing touches on her makeup. A girl couldn't look as fresh as the outdoors all the time. Sometimes she needed a little embellishment for the indoor sports.

A short breath escaped her lips as she peeked out the peephole. She still didn't feel completely safe in her house, and she hated it.

Finding Ian on her doorstep instead of a homicidal terrorist, she swung open the door and her eyes widened at the bouquet of flowers he clutched in one hand and the bottle of wine in the other. Who planned to seduce whom tonight?

He thrust forward both items. "I know you're cooking, so I figured I should contribute something."

Smiling, she took the offerings from him, musing that he had everything he needed to contribute, right in his tight jeans.

Stepping over the threshold, he cocked his head. "Something funny?"

"No. I'm just happy you remembered my favorite flower." She tilted her chin toward the bunch of lilies emitting their musky scent.

"Some things I never forget, Meg." His bottle-green gaze wandered down the length of her sweater to her legs encased in the skin-tight leggings.

She backpedaled a few steps before spinning around to locate a vase. Looked like that other part of his brain had taken over again. Made her job easy.

When she popped up clutching a glass vase from the last dozen roses Pete had sent her, Ian had shrugged out of his jacket and was sniffing the air. "You're cooking Mexican food. I always loved your cooking—straightforward, but with a kick-ass bite."

At least her cooking had been straightforward, but she didn't plan to lead him through the twists and turns of her deception again tonight. She'd have the rest of their lives for apologies, years and years to prove what a good father he could be to Travis.

If she could get him to let go of his anger.

"Is Travis sleeping?" Ian jerked his thumb toward Travis's bedroom door, open a crack.

"I picked him up late." Meg tweaked a flower petal and arranged the vase on the kitchen table. "He fell asleep in the car on the way home."

"I'm sorry. That was my fault for forcing you to take me to the upper falls."

"You hardly forced me. And I think we made an important discovery up there. Someone is definitely hiding something."

Ian's gaze shifted away from hers, and he studied the bottle of wine he still held in his hand. "I brought red. Do you think it will work with enchiladas?"

"It's red. The enchiladas are red." She shrugged. "I told you, I'm not my father's daughter."

He hoisted the bottle in the air and made for the kitchen. "Your father wouldn't be caught dead drinking the wrong wine, and mine wouldn't be caught dead wasting it. There has to be a happy medium in there somewhere."

Meg came up behind him and reached around him to open the kitchen drawer. "Maybe we're the happy medium, Ian."

He raised one brow. Then she rummaged in the drawer

for the corkscrew and dangled it from her finger. He filled two glasses with the ruby liquid and they touched rims.

Ian toasted, "To the happy medium."

The wine pooled on Meg's tongue before sliding down her throat, warming her belly. Two more sips of the fruity, tangy blend and her muscles buzzed with contentment.

She held up her index finger. "I think the enchiladas are done."

Meg brought the food to the table while Ian set out the plates and silverware. "Isn't Travis going to join us for dinner?"

"He had a late snack at Eloise's. I'm going to let him nap." Was she a bad mom to hope that Travis would sleep through the night to give her some time alone with Ian?

A quick change of expression flashed across Ian's face, too fast for Meg to read. Did he think she'd used another ploy to keep him away from his son? She had the crazy idea that she and Travis would have plenty of time to spend with Ian. Maybe Ian figured, once he found that weapon, he'd be on his way. In that case, he'd want to spend as much time as he could with Travis.

Meg bit her lip. Had she screwed up? Again?

"I—I can wake him up if you like?"

"That's okay." Ian pulled out her chair. "The little guy probably needs his sleep."

She dropped to her seat, the wine sloshing to the edge of her glass. "Oops." She licked the droplets off her fingers and grinned. It wouldn't do at all to get tipsy and try to seduce Ian. He had zero tolerance for drunks.

THEIR CONVERSATION BUBBLED throughout the meal, and Meg didn't even need to rely on the wine to loosen her tongue. The witticisms and double entendres flowed smoothly, meeting receptive and fertile ground.

Ian dabbed her lips with a napkin, touched her hand with his, plucked a lily from the vase and brushed it across her arm. If he wanted to take her on the kitchen table, she'd shove the dishes onto the floor.

Their teasing came to fruition at the kitchen sink. As she stood elbow-deep in suds, Ian approached her from behind and lifted her hair. He planted a scorching kiss on the nape of her neck. Meg tipped her head forward to invite another.

His fingers cruised through the strands of her hair as his lips continued a path up to her jaw. Her hips swayed back, and Ian wedged a knee between her legs, pressing against her backside.

A soft moan escaped Meg's lips, and she gripped the edge of the sink with soapy hands. Ian slid his hands beneath her sweater and hooked his fingers in the elastic waistband of her leggings.

He slipped one hand into the front of her leggings, toying with the edge of her panties. She gasped at the ripple of desire his touch ignited along her inner thighs. Wedging her stomach against the kitchen counter, she held up dripping hands. "No fair. I can't reach for the towel."

Growling in her ear, he said, "Don't think I'm going to get it for you."

He ground into her from behind and she felt his rock solid erection through the thin material of her leggings. As his teeth skimmed the dip between her neck and shoulder, he plunged his hand into her panties.

He shoved his hand between her legs, cupping her. She throbbed against his palm, tilting her pelvis for more contact, and hissed, "Don't be a tease."

His chuckle warmed the back of her neck, but he complied by running his finger along the length of her. She melted and folded over the sink, the ends of her hair skimming the dishwater. Her entire head could duck under the water and she wouldn't even notice, as long as Ian continued with his magic fingers.

Her breath puffed out in short spurts, sending soap bubbles airborne, where they caught the light and displayed their rainbows before dissolving. Then she squeezed her eyes shut, oblivious to the bubbles, oblivious to everything except the sweet pressure between her legs.

Her orgasm shot through her like a spear, pinning her to the counter in one long moment of breathless ecstasy before releasing the nectar from its tip, flooding her body, weakening her knees.

Ian pulled her back against his chest and then swept her up in his arms. He claimed her lips that were still soft and forming an O as the remnants of her passion popped and dissipated like those soap bubbles.

He settled on the bed next to her, peeling her leggings and underwear from her hips and sliding them down her legs. He stripped quickly, tossing his clothing over his shoulder into a messy, salacious heap.

Their foreplay had teased a hard, pulsing erection from Ian, and Meg took him in her hand and then her mouth. Moaning, Ian pulled out and kissed her lips like he owned her. She didn't even care. At this moment he did own her—body and soul.

When he entered her, Meg felt their connection like never before. She wanted Ian for Travis, but she wanted him for herself, too. She'd never stopped wanting him. She never would.

An hour later, with their passion spent, they lay side-by-side, the covers pulled up to their chins in defense against the chilly night that seemed colder after the heat they'd shared. Meg held her breath as she traced the muscles of Ian's flat belly with her fingernails. Would he jump out of bed like last time? Would the shutters fall over his eyes, blocking the light of love that gleamed from their depths?

He clenched his stomach and snorted. "That tickles."

She smiled against his shoulder, flattening her hand and rubbing circles toward his chest. "I don't want to make you laugh. You should be getting your rest if you're going to make a successful climb tomorrow."

Ian's body stiffened. Meg's hands curled into fists. *Uh-oh—here it comes.*

"I'm looking forward to it. Once I get my hands on that case, Farouk and his men will get out of Crestville for good."

Meg eased out a breath. "I'm sure Pete will be thrilled." She tapped her fingers on his chest. "And since we got sort of carried away in the kitchen, we never did discuss our plan for tomorrow. Where do you want me stationed?"

Ian's chest rose and fell beneath her hand as he filled his lungs with air and expelled it in a rush. "That's just it, Meg. I want you stationed right here. I called Buzz in to back me up."

Meg shot up, the cold air hitting her body like a blast. All this time she'd thought she was playing Ian...and he'd been playing her.

Chapter Fourteen

Ian tensed his muscles. At his announcement, Meg's mouth had dropped open, and now her jaw was working as if she couldn't quite form the words that demanded release. A few inarticulate sounds escaped from her lips before she snapped her mouth shut.

"Sorry, Meg." He stroked her arm where goose bumps dimpled her skin. "I can't put you in that kind of danger. I just found you again. I'm not going to risk the life of my son's mother."

Slumping beside him, she burrowed under the covers. "Travis needs you, too."

"I'm expendable in his life. He needs you a helluva lot more."

"Stop." She rolled to her side and braced her palm against his chest. "Don't dismiss yourself as a father, Ian. You're not expendable to Travis...or me."

Ian cinched her wrist, pressing her hand against his thundering heart. He'd expected her to go off on him for telling her what to do, for ordering her around. Instead, she was trying to convince him how important he was to Travis. Motherhood had matured her.

And what had fatherhood done for him?

"I thought..." he increased the pressure on her hand,

"I thought you'd be upset about my telling you to stay home."

She shrugged and dropped her head on his shoulder. "I know you're doing it for my safety. I get that."

He laced his fingers through hers and planted a kiss on the center of her palm. "I have a confession."

"Mmm?" Her warm mouth moved against his skin.

"Knowing I had to tell you that I'd never allow you to come with me, I seduced you. Figured it would be easier to tell you in bed than sitting across the table from you." He clenched his gut, waiting for the onslaught of indignation.

Meg giggled, and the little snorting sounds came from her nose squished against his arm. Choking, she flipped onto her back.

He drew his eyebrows over his nose, his mouth twisting into a smile. "What? Too obvious? Not obvious enough? You mean you didn't even realize I *was* seducing you?"

"I just thought I was completely irresistible." She raised her hands above her head and tousled her hair.

"Huh?" Her movement drew his gaze to her shimmering, strawberry-blond hair and desire stirred in his belly. No wonder he couldn't follow her conversation.

"I had the same plan tonight. I figured if I could seduce you, I could make you forget…"

"Forget?" The covers slipped off one perfect breast and Ian's mouth watered.

She dropped her lashes. "Forget my deceit. Forgive my terrible decision not to tell you about Travis."

Ian captured her wrists with one hand, pinning them to the headboard. His mouth hovered above hers. "I have to learn to forgive you, Meg. If I don't, how am I going to spend my life loving you?"

Her rounded eyes grew bright with tears and her lips trembled. Looked like he'd said the right thing…for once. He didn't want to blow it now, didn't want to talk anymore. Sealing his mouth over hers, he kissed his wife long and hard, as she sighed and melted beneath him.

He may not know how to be a dad yet, but he had this husband thing down.

The following morning, Ian got on the phone to Buzz, who was getting ready to board his flight. He knew he could count on his old buddy, just like Jack should know he could count on the rest of the Prospero team.

Stowing the phone in his pocket, Ian sauntered into the kitchen and tugged on Travis's hair.

Travis yelled, "Hey," and batted away his hand.

Ian crouched down and went nose-to-nose with his son. "For the amount of sleep you had, you should be in a better mood."

Meg laughed and slid a plate of scrambled eggs on the table. "Are you hungry?"

"I'm always hungry." He wasn't even trying to seduce her, but every comment and every touch brought a hint of rose to her cheeks.

She brushed her hands together and placed them on her hips. "What time are you going up today?"

"As soon as Buzz gets here. We should be ready to roll by this afternoon."

"I hope that suitcase is still there when you get up to that ledge."

Ian speared a clump of egg. "We don't know for sure it's there, and if it is, Farouk's guy hasn't been successful in getting to it yet. I'm going to hike out and keep an eye on that cliff face this morning anyway."

"Good idea." She wiped Travis's mouth with a damp cloth and unhooked the tray from his high chair. "If you think of any more equipment you might need, let me know. I'm going in to Rocky Mountain Adventures today to catch up on that paperwork I missed out on yesterday. All hikes are canceled for the week though, so it should be slow. I expect just Richard to be in the office today."

"Keep Richard close and don't go hiking on your own. Are you going to check up on Matt?"

"Yeah, his girlfriend should be back in town. I'll give her a call." She swung Travis out of his high chair and hitched him on her hip. "Are you ready?"

Travis nodded and then held his arms out to Ian, who half rose from his chair. "Should I...does he want...?"

"He wants you to hold him. He was pretty excited to see you here this morning—not traumatized at all." She winked, showing she'd seen through his excuse to hightail it out of her bedroom the other morning.

Ian stumbled to his feet, nearly knocking over the kitchen chair. He reached across the table and Travis stretched toward him. Ian plucked him from Meg's arms, and the boy burrowed into his shoulder. Inhaling the scent of him—baby shampoo and sticky hands—Ian squeezed Travis's soft body against his hard chest.

Travis squirmed, bumping his head on Ian's chin, where his beard caught strands of Travis's brown hair. Travis leaned back in Ian's arms and opened and closed his hands.

"That's bye-bye." Meg slung Travis's backpack over her shoulder. "Can you say, 'bye-bye, Daddy?'"

Travis repeated it in his high, clear voice, "Bye-bye, Daddy," and that's all it took for Ian's throat to tighten. He thrust Travis back into Meg's waiting arms.

She kissed Ian's mouth and whispered, "You're doing great."

He held the door open for her. "I'll give you a call when Buzz gets here, and then I'll give you another call when it's all over. In the meantime, stay put at the office or at home."

"Gotcha, boss." She leaned in closer and cupped the side of his face with one hand. "You be careful up there. I'll be waiting for your call."

As she strode to her car, she pointed to the steel-gray sky. "It's going to snow today."

Rubbing his unshaved chin, Ian watched Meg pull away. He'd return to his hotel room, prepare for his climb and then stake out the cliff. Then he'd tackle the really hard part—preparing to be a husband again—a good one this time—and shouldering the awesome responsibility of parenthood.

WHEN MEG REACHED Eloise's Day Care, Eloise was scurrying around the rooms, picking up toys and stacking blocks.

Her daughter Felicia rolled her eyes at Meg. "She always gets like this when prospective parents drop by." Felicia cupped her hands around her mouth. "Hey, Mom, the kids are just going to mess it up anyway, and if that couple is going to carry on like they did yesterday, they won't notice anyway."

Meg laughed, glad that Travis might have another toddler to play with—hopefully another talkative girl. She waved to Travis and took off for the Rocky Mountain Adventures office.

When she walked into the office, Richard looked up from a mountain climbing magazine. He ducked back behind the pages. "Scared me for a minute. I thought you might be another irate tourist."

"It's a good time to cancel hikes anyway." Meg jerked

her thumb over her shoulder. "I think it's going to snow today."

"Early snow, good ski season, more money."

"You have your priorities straight." She hitched her backpack on a hook by the door. "Any news about Matt?"

"No, but Ali is back. We'll get more out of her than Sheriff Cahill."

Meg blew out a breath and hunched over her desk. As Richard flipped through the pages of his magazine, Meg powered on her computer and started processing refunds.

AN HOUR LATER, the office phone rang and Richard picked it up after trying to ignore it for five rings. "Yeah, hold on." He held up the phone. "It's Ian Dempsey, for you, and I'm going out on the trail for a while. I'm going stir-crazy in here."

As Richard dropped the phone on her desk, Meg checked the time on the computer. Buzz couldn't have made it here that fast. Maybe Ian saw something on his surveillance, but he was supposed to stop in before heading out.

"Ian? Everything okay?" She swallowed, as uneasiness tickled the back of her neck.

"Everything's fine. I tried you on your cell phone, but you didn't pick up. Buzz isn't here yet, but I wanted to share some interesting information with you that I got from Colonel Scripps. Luckily, he caught me before I started hiking down into the gorge."

Meg clutched the phone. "What?"

"Hans Birnbacher must've been in the wrong place at the wrong time, or he tried to scam the wrong people. Turns out the cops in Phoenix and in Albuquerque picked him up for trying to run some con. He was supposed to leave the country, but he wasn't detained and he slipped through the cracks."

"That's comforting to know." Meg released a shaky breath and strolled to her backpack to retrieve her cell phone. "What does that have to do with his death?"

"Who knows? Maybe he saw something. Maybe he figured this was his big break, but he had no idea who he was dealing with."

"I can almost feel sorry for the guy." She dropped her phone on the desk and then dropped back in her chair.

"Yeah, but there's more."

Meg's fingers, which had been tapping the desk, froze. "More?"

"The police in Colorado Springs discovered a couple murdered in their hotel room."

Meg gasped and gripped the edge of the desk with damp fingers. Her pulse throbbed in her temple as a shaft of pain shot through her. "Wh-what does that mean?"

"It means we had the wrong tourists all along."

Meg waited, her throat too dry to eke out a simple question.

"Are you still there, Meg?"

She managed an animal noise, something between a groan and a whimper.

"The names of the dead couple were Russ and Jeanine Taylor. Do you remember that pair on the hike? The supposedly honeymooning couple, all lovey-dovey?"

"Uh-huh."

"They're the ones, Meg. They killed Kayla and then they killed Birnbacher. But first they killed the real Russ and Jeanine Taylor to steal their identities and get on that hike."

New couple. Lovey-dovey. Affectionate.

Meg's head felt stuck in a fog. Her tongue grew thick and mute in her mouth.

"Are you all right? I know it's a shock. They must've had the same idea as Kayla and I had—show up as a couple, deflect suspicion. I just want to know where they've been hiding out all this time. Probably figured it was only a matter of time before the police in Colorado Springs found the Taylors' bodies."

She swallowed and drove her fingers into her temple. "Ian. Eloise told me that a new couple was looking at the day care for their daughter."

"Yeah, so?" He sucked in a sharp breath. "So what, Meg? Lots of couples shop around for day care."

The pain was dancing around her head now, with pinpoints of light stabbing her eyes. "Eloise and her daughter both described the couple as very affectionate and lovey-dovey, more like honeymooners than parents shopping for day care. Sound familiar?"

Ian's voice rasped across the phone. "Call Eloise now. Do it on your cell phone. I'll wait on the office phone."

Meg's fear solidified and lodged like a boulder in her belly. She'd wanted Ian to shrug off her anxiety and suspicions, dismiss them as the loony ravings of an overprotective mother. But he'd taken her seriously. He saw the same possibility that loomed in her imagination.

"Hang on." She placed the office phone on the desk and picked up her cell.

Eloise answered after three rings. Meg took a deep breath to steady her vibrating nerves. "Hi, Eloise. It's Meg O'Reilly. I'm just calling to check on Travis."

"Travis is down for his nap in the back room, Meg. Did you want to speak to him?"

"No. I thought he had a little runny nose this morning. Did that couple come to check out the day care?"

Eloise sniffed. "They came. Didn't bring their daughter though, and they were very picky. Looked into everything."

"They're gone now?" Meg's blood still raced through her veins and she had to close her eyes against the dizziness that threatened to lay her out.

"They left just a little while ago, and I have to say I'm glad. I didn't care for them at all."

Meg flattened a hand on her belly and squeezed her eyes. "What were their names, Eloise?"

"Taylor. Russ and Jeanine."

Meg's stomach rolled and she gritted her teeth, nausea sweeping through her body like an avalanche. With her chest heaving, Meg covered her heart with one shaky hand. "Eloise, can you please check on Travis for me? Just have a look at him."

"Okay, dear, but he didn't seem sick at all to me this morning."

Meg could hear babies fussing and the voices of other children, as Eloise moved through the playrooms toward the nap room in the back of the house. The nap room with the side door leading to the gravel driveway that curved from the front of the house.

Eloise whispered, "He's in the corner with his favorite blanket."

Just as Meg began to slump in the chair and grab the office phone to give Ian the good news, Eloise's voice came back sharply. "Travis is gone."

Adrenaline pumped through Meg's system, propelling her out of her seat. She clutched both phones in her hands and yelled into one. "Are you sure, Eloise? Look in the other cots."

The other phone scorched her hand, as Ian barked out

questions over the line. She couldn't bring herself to tell him the son he'd just discovered had been kidnapped.

Eloise's voice caught. "I can't find him, Meg. Maybe he got out of the nap room and wandered into another part of the house."

Meg's breath came out in short spurts. *Or maybe the Taylors kidnapped him.*

"Please, Eloise…" Meg's voice trailed off as "Russ Taylor" sauntered through the front door of the office, pointing a gun at her.

Chapter Fifteen

Ian's voice squawked over the office phone, and Meg shoved it behind the computer's keyboard and pressed the speaker button with stiff fingers. She had to let Ian know what was happening, but she'd have to keep the open line a secret from the man with the gun.

She had her cell phone on speaker also, and now Eloise's voice strained across the line. "Meg, do you want me to call the police?"

The man sliced a finger across his throat and whispered, "Tell that old witch the boy's safe."

Meg nodded. "Eloise? I'm sorry. I just got a call from Travis's father. He took Travis. He doesn't know the rules."

Eloise let out a gush of air. "Oh my God, Meg. You had my heart racing. If your husband is going to stick around, please explain protocol to him."

Meg ended the call and placed her cell phone in the middle of the desk. "I told her. Now what do you want from me?"

She couldn't hear Ian's voice over the line anymore, but hopefully he'd caught on and could hear her.

The man took a step forward. "It's simple, Meg. I want you to do a little rock climbing for me, so I can claim what's mine and be on my way."

"Can you get that gun out of my face?"

"Would you prefer a knife?"

Meg gasped. "Matt. Why'd you attack Matt?"

"I had the same simple request of him, but he refused me. You won't be foolish enough to refuse me, will you Meg? After all, I have Travis as collateral. Matt's girlfriend was out of town, so I couldn't use her."

She trained her gaze away from the open phone line near the computer, but said a silent prayer. "Is that why you've been hanging around Crestville? You've been waiting for someone to retrieve the case?"

"I'm not a rock climber."

"Where is it? Maybe nobody can get it now." She'd have to pretend she didn't know the location of the suitcase or he'd figure Ian knew its location.

"That's not what Matt told me...when he was still talking. He said people lead climb and solo climb that rock face all the time."

"Kayla saw the suitcase that first day on the hike, didn't she?" Meg whispered.

The man edged closer to the desk, keeping his weapon pointed in her general direction. "We came upon her on the lookout, with her binoculars zeroed-in on our suitcase. We knew where it had fallen since we'd enclosed a tracking device in the case. We offered to take her picture and then pushed her over."

"And what about the German tourist?"

The man laughed, a booming sound that made Meg flinch. "He tried to blackmail us. Can you believe that?" He muttered something in another language... Russian?

"Who *are* you?"

"You can call me Mike. It's closer to my real name than Russ."

"Where's my son, Mike?" Meg tried to speak directly into the phone. Then she held her breath, hoping the man wouldn't notice.

"He's with my lovely wife." Mike chuckled. "I'll give her the all-clear to release him when you make that climb and hand over our property."

"No." A plan was forming in Meg's mind, bit by bit. As long as Ian was still on the other end of that line listening, it just might work.

Mike's eyebrows shot up and he steadied his weapon. "No?"

"Your lovely wife is going to bring Travis to our location, or at least a safe place where I can see him from where we are. The suitcase is near the upper falls, isn't it?"

"How do you know that?"

She shrugged. "It makes sense now. Kayla had a clear view of the area from the lookout, and that cliff face is just about the only place for rock climbing in the entire gorge."

"And you want my partner to bring your son to the gorge? Even Katrina can't hike down there carrying a child."

"I wouldn't want her to try. There's an easy trail above the falls. We can see it from the gorge. Have her bring Travis there after parking in the turnout at highway marker twenty-five."

His eyes flickered with recognition. Of course he'd been on that trail. He'd been there when he covered his suitcase with branches and leaves.

"I'm going to have to see my son alive and well before I give you the suitcase, or I'm not going to make the climb at all."

The man narrowed his eyes. "What kind of game are you playing, Meg?"

"I need to know my son is okay. What are you going to do, Mike? Keep killing people until you find a rock climber to get your case, or call in one of your terrorist buddies who won't get within a hundred yards of that rock?"

"Where's your CIA protector?" He straightened his back, widening his stance.

Meg snorted. "He's not my protector. Like you said, he's CIA, doing his job. He doesn't care about my son. All he wants is that suitcase."

"Where is he?"

"He went to pick up another agent. They're going to scour that area, and sooner or later they're going to figure out the location of the case."

"Then we'd better get moving."

"My son?" Meg folded her arms across her chest where her heart beat a wild staccato. She had to keep it together.

"He'll be there. Now come out from behind that desk and get the equipment you'll need before your coworker returns. We've left enough dead bodies in this backwater town."

Did you get that, Ian? Travis will be there. And you need to save him.

IAN CLENCHED THE steering wheel of his rental car and released a breath. As soon as he'd heard Meg's words to Eloise on the other line, he knew Travis was in trouble. He'd been able to follow most of the conversation between her and the man who called himself "Mike"— Mikhail most likely, judging from his accent.

As far as Prospero knew, Farouk, who'd been responsible for securing the money for this deal, had always worked with the big-name terrorist groups in the Mideast. If he now had ties to the Russians, this must be some kind of United Nations of terrorist cells. And that meant bad news for everyone.

When the fact of Travis's kidnapping had sunk in, failure washed over Ian like a tide of brackish water. He'd flunked the most basic tenet of parenthood—keeping your child safe. But he had a chance now to make everything right. Meg had given him that chance, and he wouldn't fail her. He wouldn't fail Travis.

Once he rescued his son, he'd have to rescue Meg. Ian needed to get Travis out of the area while he finished his work. He called Eloise's Day Care and told a mystified Felicia, Eloise's daughter, to meet him at the trailhead that led to the upper falls.

Then he got on the phone to Buzz to relay the new plan. Ian would need backup, and he couldn't think of anyone he'd rather have on his side than one of his buddies from Prospero, especially a pilot like Buzz, who could fly a chopper in the most dangerous situations— like this one.

ABOUT AN HOUR LATER, after securing Felicia at the still empty Rocky Mountain Adventures office, Ian crouched behind a clump of bushes that bordered the trail above the upper falls. When he'd passed highway marker twenty-five, he hadn't seen any cars there, which meant he'd gotten there before Mike's partner.

By now Meg had to be in the gorge with Mike, waiting for Travis's appearance. And Ian had a nice surprise waiting for Mike's wife when she showed up.

A scuffling sound and the crack of a twig had Ian coiling his muscles and rising to his haunches. He could take down a woman easy enough, but he didn't want to harm his son in the process.

The woman appeared on the trail, and Ian clenched his fists as he saw Travis in a sling across her chest, fashioned from some kind of sheet. He couldn't see Travis's face, but his little legs were kicking up a storm. *That's right, buddy, give her hell.*

The woman stopped a few feet from Ian's hiding place, and he held his breath.

"Stop kicking and I'll let you see your mommy through the binoculars. You want to see your mommy, don't you?"

"Where's my mommy?"

Ian's heart lurched at the sob in Travis's voice.

She scooped a phone from the pocket of her jacket. "Mikhail, we're here." She waved an arm over her head. "Can you see us?"

She paused, and then, "Yes, yes, I'll turn the brat around so she can see him. Why did you agree to this? It's lunacy, and Farouk is not going to like it. That's why we grabbed the boy. She'd have to make the climb or we'd kill him."

Ian could almost believe the woman could hear his teeth gnashing.

She fumbled with the bunched-up sling and grabbed Travis under the arms as she lifted him over her head. "Do you see your mommy down there? She's just leading my friend on a hike. Nothing to worry about."

Travis bicycled his legs, his heel banging the woman's forehead. "I want my daddy."

Ian's chest tightened. *Your daddy's right here, Travis. And he's going to protect you forever.*

"Is she satisfied, Mikhail? I'll be more than happy to turn over this kid when we get the case."

Apparently, the appearance of Travis did satisfy Meg, because the woman dropped her phone back into her pocket and began to wrestle a squirming Travis back into the sling.

"Walk. Walk."

Ian eased out a breath. Maybe Travis sensed his presence, because it would be a helluva lot easier to take down this woman if she didn't have his son tied to her body.

"I'll gladly let you walk, but you'd better hold my hand, because if you take a dive over the edge, the deal's off."

The tall woman hunched slightly as she gripped Travis's hand and moved away from the edge of the cliff. They shuffled down the trail and adrenaline pumped through Ian's system.

Filling his lungs with air, he launched from his hiding place, going airborne. He saw the woman's wide eyes and open mouth as she looked over her shoulder before he tackled her from behind. She released Travis's hand and went for her pocket. Ian smashed his knee against her wrist and she cried out in pain.

Jerking his head up, he caught sight of Travis, his mittened hands covering his mouth. "Sit down on the rock, Travis. It's okay."

When he had the woman pinned to the ground, the side of her face mashed into the dirt, he plunged his hand in her pocket and pulled out a gun. With one hand, he released the chamber and spilled the bullets on the ground.

He reached into her other pocket and grabbed her cell phone. He chucked it against a rock where it broke apart. He didn't have any rope to tie her up and he didn't want to shoot her in front of Travis. Shifting his body to block Travis's view, Ian slammed the woman's gun against the back of her head.

Blood spurted from the wound and Ian dragged her from the trail into the bushes. Not that he expected anyone on this trail, with Rocky Mountain Adventures closed and the skies threatening snow.

Wiping his hands on his jeans, he turned to Travis, who was wide-eyed and silent. Ian's gut twisted. He never wanted Travis to witness his violence. Would his son shrink from him now...the way Ian shrank from his own father after one of his rages?

Ian dropped to his knees and held his arms wide. "Everything's okay now, Travis."

Ian's heart hammered painfully against his ribs as Travis watched him from beneath lowered lashes. Then Travis jumped from the rock and flung himself against Ian's chest.

With his throat tight and his eyes squeezed shut, Ian stroked his son's soft curls. "You're going to be fine, Travis."

Now I have to save your mother.

THE SIGHT OF TRAVIS on the ridge had eased the tightness in Meg's chest. Would they keep their word and release him once she made this climb? She didn't have any other choice but to trust them.

But she trusted Ian more.

Mike hadn't realized the phone next to the computer was an open line, or that she'd pressed the speaker button as soon as she laid eyes on the gun in his hand. She hadn't heard Ian's voice over the phone, so hopefully he'd caught on quickly, and was privy to the conversation. She'd stayed behind the desk to make Mike come to her, not that she could've moved her leaden legs anyway.

She hoped Eloise had accepted her lame explanation of Travis's disappearance from the nap room. She didn't need Pete Cahill swarming all over town, looking for Travis and putting his life in jeopardy. Mike and Katrina, he'd called her "Katrina," must've unlocked the dead bolt on the back door in the nap room that led to the side of the house, and then crept around later to kidnap Travis.

"Okay, you've seen your son. Let's get down to business." Mike pointed up. "Do you see that ledge with the greenery? My property is right up there. You can do it, can't you Meg? Even with your sore shoulder?"

She narrowed her eyes. "Why did you try to kill me if you needed my help? Or did you think you'd be getting Matt to help you?"

Raising his dark eyebrows, he shrugged. "I wasn't trying to kill you, Meg. I was trying to kill the CIA agent—who might be on his way as we speak, so let's get going."

Meg swallowed. "Well, you're a lousy shot." She perched on a granite boulder and untied her boots to slip on a pair of climbing shoes.

He handed her a radio. "Take this so we can have some communication when you get to the top. I want to know the condition of the case when you reach it. It should be concealed with some branches and leaves."

She slipped the radio in the front pocket of her vest and then stepped into her harness. She fed a length of rope through a self-locking device on the harness.

Mike studied her from his deep-set eyes. "How are you going to get my case back down?"

Meg nudged a coil of rope and bungee cords with her toe. "I can strap it to my back. How heavy is it?"

"It's not heavy at all."

His answer surprised her. She didn't have any idea what constituted a trigger for a nuclear device, but she figured it would be heavy. "What's in the suitcase, Mike?"

His lips flattened against his teeth. "That's not your concern, Meg. Just know it's not dangerous on its own."

"Okay, Mike. I trust you." She sneered, trying to match his expression. If she'd seen that look on his face just once while he and his fake wife were on her hike, she'd have pegged him as evil from the outset.

Would've saved everyone a whole lot of trouble.

IAN STRETCHED OUT flat on his belly, a few feet from the edge of where the cliff dropped off to the ledge that was Meg's target.

From his vantage point, Ian had watched Meg make her steady climb up the cliff face. She climbed swiftly and surely, despite the increasing snow flurries and her injured shoulder.

From below, Mike held his gun on her ascending form, although how he thought she'd escape from that sheer wall of rock, Ian couldn't fathom.

Meg had a few more feet before she hoisted herself over the edge and reached the suitcase. Ian scooted closer to the edge, shielded by the scrubby bushes that clung to the side of the mountain.

When he saw Meg's face, he called out, "Meg. I'm here."

Her hand faltered for a moment before her face broke into a smile that could melt the snow. It melted Ian's heart, anyway.

She twisted her head over her shoulder. "Mike can't see you, can he? They have Travis here somewhere."

"I have Travis, Meg. I took him from Mike's partner after she showed him to you. I heard your entire conversation with Mike."

Her smile got even bigger as she reached for the next handhold. "Where is he?"

"He's safe with Felicia at your house. He's fine. How's your shoulder holding up?"

"Thank God…and you, Ian. My shoulder's fine, but Mike will be expecting his suitcase down there. Even though he no longer has Travis to hold over my head, how am I going to get down with Mike waiting for me with a gun?"

"Don't worry about that. I have it all worked out. Come on now, just a few more feet and you're home free. If you hadn't already started the climb by the time I got back from securing Travis, I could've saved you the ordeal."

She exhaled and grinned. "I do this for fun. It's no ordeal."

"You're a stud, Meg-o." He should've known she'd have his back. He should've always known that.

Her head became level with the lip of the ledge and she hoisted herself over, landing on the flat surface of rock. Like a conquering hero, she rose to her feet and waved her hands above her head, signaling to Mike that she'd made it.

Not that it was going to do him any good now.

Her radio crackled and Mike said, "Check the suitcase."

"Good idea." She rolled her eyes at Ian. Crouching down, she brushed the branches and debris from a hard-sided carry-on-size suitcase. "Mike was right. It *is* light."

Ian frowned. "It's light? Is it still intact? Maybe it broke and lost its contents in the fall."

Meg ran her hands around the edge of the case. "It's intact...and locked."

"Is it okay? Is it okay?" Mike's voice rattled across the radio.

Ignoring Mike, Meg set the case down and opened and closed her hands, stretching her fingers. "What now, Ian?"

Pointing to the sky, he said, "We wait for Buzz."

"Buzz is dropping from the heavens, or what?"

The sound of thwacking blades answered Meg's question. Buzz to the rescue, and right on time.

Meg's mouth dropped open. "Didn't you tell him it was dangerous to fly a helicopter up here?"

"Sure I told him. That's how I convinced him to do it."

Mike's frantic voice crackled and hissed. "What's going on? What's that chopper doing here? I told you, Meg, no funny business. We have your son. One phone call to Katrina and he's dead."

Meg pushed the button on the radio with a deliberate finger. "You're mistaken, Mike. Katrina doesn't have my son, and I'm afraid there's going to be a *lot* of funny business."

She chucked the radio off the cliff where it bounced on the rocks below. Turning to look up at Ian, she said, "What do you want me to do?"

"Can you strap that suitcase on your back?"

"No problem. That's what I had in mind for my descent."

Gunshots rang from the canyon below, and Meg ducked. "Can he hit us from down there?"

Ian stretched to his full height. "No. We're safe

up here, unless he pulls out a rocket launcher for the chopper."

While Meg fed a rope through the handle of the suitcase, Ian waved his arms at Buzz, hovering closely to the big rocks that jutted out from the side of the mountain.

Ian knew, if anyone could handle this mission, it was Buzz.

Someone riding in the chopper with Buzz lowered a ladder over the ledge where Meg bravely stood, legs apart, case strapped to her back. Ian wished he could be in her place, but he knew Meg could handle it.

"Grab the ladder, Meg."

Ian's jaw ached with tension as he watched Meg climb the swaying ladder one rung at a time. He didn't take a breath until Buzz's partner pulled her into the chopper.

Then Buzz edged the chopper to Ian's position. As Ian reached for the ladder, he heard a movement behind him. With one hand on the first rung of the ladder, he twisted around. Katrina, blood streaming down the side of her face, charged him with a knife clutched in her hand.

Ian released the ladder to reach for his gun. A shot rang out from the chopper and Katrina dropped to the ground and rolled off the cliff, her body taking the place of the suitcase she'd so desperately wanted.

Ian looked up to see Buzz leveling his weapon out the window of the helicopter. Buzz nodded once.

Just like old times.

MEG FINALLY RELEASED her hold on Ian when Buzz touched the chopper down on the landing pad next to the Rocky Mountain Adventures office. When she saw Katrina coming at Ian with a knife, her heart had leaped into her throat, strangling all sound. Luckily, Buzz had seen Katrina, too, and was able to fire his weapon out the window.

Ian had radioed the sheriff's department to take care of Mike, but they hadn't heard anything yet. The madness wasn't over, and the tension of the day still had a grip on Meg's neck.

Dylan, Buzz's buddy, whom he'd snagged from the Schriever Air Force Base, hopped out of the chopper first, followed by Ian, who helped her out.

Once Buzz had secured the chopper, they all clambered into the empty Rocky Mountain Adventures office.

Buzz hoisted the battered case onto a desk and opened the top drawer. "Do you have a letter opener in here?"

Ian's cell phone rang and he glanced at the display. "It's Cahill. I'm going to put him on speaker."

Meg handed a letter opener to Buzz as Ian talked into the phone. "Do you have him, Sheriff Cahill?"

"We got him, Dempsey, and then he took some kind of suicide pill. Croaked right in front of us."

Ian swore. "Did he say anything before he offed himself?"

"Not much of interest to us. He rambled about having others, and when we told him his partner in crime was dead, he seemed to think that was pretty funny."

"Funny?"

"Yeah, he said something about Katrina being some guy's girlfriend, and how Prospero would pay for her death."

Meg clutched her hands in front of her, twisting her fingers. Was Ian still in danger?

Ian exchanged a look with Buzz. "What was the guy's name, Cahill? Do you remember?"

"I didn't completely catch it."

"Could it have been Farouk?"

"Yeah, sure. It could've been. Is this business over now, Dempsey? Do you boys have what you want?"

Ian quirked an eyebrow at Buzz. "It's never over, Sheriff, but it's over for Crestville. Your residents can start getting ready for ski season in peace."

Ian ended the call and blew out a breath. "Katrina was Farouk's girlfriend?"

Buzz shook his head as he worked on the lock. "This is looking more and more like Farouk's own operation. He's not working for anyone else. He's the boss this time, and the boss is going to be in a rage when he learns about his girlfriend.

The lock clicked and Buzz said, "Got it."

Meg squeezed in between the two men as Buzz flipped the latches of the old-style suitcase and raised the lid.

Ian stiffened beside her and Buzz slammed his fist on the desk so hard the little vials in the sealed plastic trembled.

"Wh-what are they?" She wrinkled her nose at the cushioned case fitted in the bottom, with a clear box lined with narrow vials containing...nothing.

Ian ground out through clenched teeth. "Farouk is playing with fire...biological weapons of mass destruction."

Meg stumbled back. "Is it dangerous like that, contained in those vials?"

"Not in that hermetically sealed plastic box. And if that didn't break getting tossed out of an airplane, we're safe."

Buzz scratched his chin. "We thought it was a trigger, or device of some sort. What does Farouk plan to do with this? And what exactly *is* this?"

Ian tapped the label affixed to the plastic case. "Look, it says 'H1N9.' It must be some kind of mutated flu virus. We need to turn it over to the Centers for Disease Control. How exactly does biological warfare connect to plans to assassinate Okeke? And where does Jack fit in?"

Buzz snapped his fingers. "Jack's last job before he disappeared concerned some doctor, didn't it? Doctor... virus...maybe we're getting warmer."

"I don't like it, Buzz. Look how close that madman got to Meg and Travis, and now it's personal, isn't it? You killed Katrina. Farouk's never going to forget that."

"That's my problem." Buzz clapped Ian on the shoulder. "I'm heading back to D.C., and then New York next week."

Ian gestured toward the case. "Do you think this is it?"

"Not by a long shot. Mike admitted, before he killed himself, that they had more." Buzz snapped the case shut. "Like you told the sheriff, it's never over."

A few hours later, as she and Ian stepped through the front door of her house, Meg ran to Travis and scooped him into her arms. She sent Felicia home with many thanks and few explanations.

Ian didn't want to leave Travis's side, and insisted on giving him a bath. With water splashing in the background, Meg checked her voice mail. She smiled. Matt had regained consciousness and was out of danger.

Meg replaced the phone and chewed her bottom lip. Were any of them out of danger as long as people like Farouk plied their trade?

"Hey, this is one clean boy." Ian strode into the living room, carrying Travis wrapped in a towel, his damp head poking out of the top.

"Everything okay?" Ian wedged a finger beneath Meg's chin.

Her lips slid into a smile. "Matt's doing better."

"But Meg isn't?"

"I'm worried about..." Her arms flailed at her sides encompassing everything.

Ian hitched Travis on his hip and pulled Meg close, his warm breath stirring the wild strands of her hair. "You have nothing to worry about, Meg Dempsey. I'm here with you now and I always will be. I'm not afraid anymore."

He kissed Travis's soft, rosy cheek and then pressed his lips against hers. "You can lean on me, and I'll lean on you, too."

She wrapped her arms around her husband's waist, trapping their son between them. She had her husband back, and with him by her side, she had nothing to fear.

Epilogue

A cold blast of apprehension whooshed down his back as the sounds of the village, teeming with people, reached his ears. It had seemed smaller from his mountain perch.

He ducked behind some scrubby bushes and adjusted the cloth around his neck to cover his head and lower face. He sucked in a sharp breath as pain knifed between his shoulders. The arduous walk from the mountains had taxed his battered body.

He had no idea what he was walking into. His location in the mountains, where he'd awakened on that ledge, would indicate that he'd come from this village. Why had no one looked for him?

Maybe someone in the village had put him there.

He put his head down and shuffled toward the village streets. The voices rose around him as he trudged toward the center of the village, marked by colorful stalls and bustling people.

He understood their words. He thought in English, he spoke in English, but he knew this language. The people around him argued, bargained, joked.

He stooped his shoulders more as he came to realize he towered over most of the people in the bazaar. A persistent feeling of being watched had him pulling the head cloth closely around his face.

Could he ask the residents of this town his identity? Could he ask them for help? Or would they send him back to his cold, hard bed in the mountains?

Dipping his hand into the pocket of his loose pants, he scrambled for the coins he'd felt on his trek down from the mountain. He could buy some hot, sweet tea. Sit down and think.

He turned the corner off the main square. Someone jumped at him from between two buildings and he spun around and pulled the person against his chest, his arm locked around his throat in a move so natural it felt scripted.

The slight figure in his grip struggled and choked, and he realized he'd overpowered a boy. He released his captive, but tensed his muscles, ready to renew his assault if the boy attacked him.

The boy turned slowly, his dark eyes wide. "Why did you grab me like that, Mister Jack?"

* * * * *

Don't miss Buzz's story,
as Carol Ericson's miniseries,
BROTHERS IN ARMS, continues.
Look for it wherever
Harlequin Intrigue books are sold!

Harlequin

INTRIGUE

COMING NEXT MONTH

Available May 10, 2011

#1275 BABY BOOTCAMP
Daddy Corps
Mallory Kane

#1276 BRANDED
Whitehorse, Montana: Chisholm Cattle Company
B.J. Daniels

#1277 DAMAGED
Colby Agency: The New Equalizers
Debra Webb

#1278 THE MAN FROM GOSSAMER RIDGE
Cooper Justice: Cold Case Investigation
Paula Graves

#1279 UNFORGETTABLE
Cassie Miles

#1280 BEAR CLAW CONSPIRACY
Bear Claw Creek Crime Lab
Jessica Andersen

HICNM0411

REQUEST YOUR FREE BOOKS!
2 FREE NOVELS PLUS 2 FREE GIFTS!

◆ Harlequin®

INTRIGUE®

BREATHTAKING ROMANTIC SUSPENSE

*With an evil force hell-bent on destruction,
two enemies must unite to find a truth that turns
all-too-personal when passions collide.*

*Enjoy a sneak peek in Jenna Kernan's next installment
in her original* TRACKER *series, GHOST STALKER,
available in May, only from Harlequin Nocturne.*

"**W**ho are you?" he snarled.

Jessie lifted her chin. "Your better."

His smile was cold. "Such arrogance could only come from a Niyanoka."

She nodded. "Why are you here?"

"I don't know." He glanced about her room. "I asked the birds to take me to a healer."

"And they have done so. Is that *all* you asked?"

"No. To lead them away from my friends." His eyes fluttered and she saw them roll over white.

Jessie straightened, preparing to flee, but he roused himself and mastered the momentary weakness. His eyes snapped open, locking on her.

Her heart hammered as she inched back.

"Lead who away?" she whispered, suddenly afraid of the answer.

"The ghosts. Nagi sent them to attack me so I would bring them to her."

The wolf must be deranged because Nagi did not send ghosts to attack living creatures. He captured the evil ones after their death if they refused to walk the Way of Souls, forcing them to face judgment.

"Her? The healer you seek is also female?"

"Michaela. She's Niyanoka, like you. The last Seer of Souls and Nagi wants her dead."

Jessie fell back to her seat on the carpet as the possibility of this ricocheted in her brain. Could it be true?

"Why should I believe you?" But she knew why. His black aura, the part that said he had been touched by death. Only a ghost could do that. But it made no sense.

Why would Nagi hunt one of her people and why would a Skinwalker want to protect her? She had been trained from birth to hate the Skinwalkers, to consider them a threat.

His intent blue eyes pinned her. Jessie felt her mouth go dry as she considered the impossible. Could the trickster be speaking the truth? Great Mystery, what evil was this?

She stared in astonishment. There was only one way to find her answers. But she had never even met a Skinwalker before and so did not even know if they dreamed.

But if he dreamed, she would have her chance to learn the truth.

Look for GHOST STALKER by Jenna Kernan, available May only from Harlequin Nocturne, wherever books and ebooks are sold.